THE LAST OF ONE

STEPHAN SOLBERG

Pocol Press
Clifton, VA

POCOL PRESS

Published in the United States of America
by Pocol Press
6023 Pocol Drive
Clifton VA 20124
www.pocolpress.com

Publisher's Cataloguing-in-Publication

Solberg, Stephan

    The last of one / Stephan Solberg. – 1st ed. –   Clifton, VA : Pocol
Press, c2010.

    p.; cm.

    ISBN: 978-1-929763-46-7

    1. World War, 1914-1918—Fiction. 2. History, Modern—20th
century—Fiction. 3. United States—History—20th century—Fiction. 4.
Older people—Fiction. 5. Aging—Fiction. I. Title.

PS3619.O432 L37 2010
813.6--dc22   1004

Cover art by the author. Author photograph by Daniel Solberg.

Dedication

This book is dedicated to my great-uncle Corporal Percival H. Solberg of the 73rd Company, 6th Regiment, U.S.M.C., who fought in WWI. He died from a wound inflicted just one day before the Armistice was signed to end the war.

Also, to my late father Lawrence J. Solberg who always loved history and taught it for over thirty years.

Acknowledgments

Special thanks to my sister Lynne Perry for entrusting me with the letters and diary of our great-uncle Percy.

I am fortunate and grateful to have a superb editor in my wife, Victoria Everitt.   Thanks, Angel.

God bless you, Frank Buckles.

Several books and articles were researched for this story, including:

Miracle at Belleau Wood: The Birth of the Modern U.S. Marine Corps by Alan Axelrod, Lyons Press, 2007;

The Battle of Belleau Wood—A First Hand Account by Colonel Frederick May Wise, Lucent Books, 1996; and

"Going In" The Grueling Night March to Soissons by Pvt. Louis C. Linn, Miltary History Quarterly, 2003.

Also, thanks to the Aurora, Illinois Public Library, and the Robert R. McCormick Library and First Division Museum in Winfield, Illinois.

Prologue

...The old man is dreaming again.

It is a dream from long ago that he'd had many times over the years, more years than most people live to remember. Each time it is a little different, but each time he thinks it is exactly the same. He is sixteen years old and lying in the middle of a field of tall, green wheat. It is June, and the seed on the wheat is full and ripening, the sun is high, and the air is thick with the smell of life. Lying next to him is a woman he has always and only loved. Her name is Helen, and her dark eyes look lovingly into his as he touches her hair that reminds him of the color of prairie grass in autumn. They'd just made love, and he now caresses her stomach as they laugh and talk and imagine a life together. He picks a red poppy that is growing in the wheat and tenderly places it behind her ear. It echoes the color in her cheeks and lips. She smiles and kisses him. They look out towards the lake named after the Indian word for 'big water.' This is in their hometown in Wisconsin on the shore of Lake Michigan, and, on a day such as this, the sky and water become one.

A rumbling sound is now heard in the distance, like an approaching storm. As he looks across the field, he sees four horses running straight at them. Though the field looks the same, he isn't back home anymore but is now in France, in the Marne Valley. The year is 1918. The horses are wearing masks that cover their eyes like big bubbles and their mouths and noses with dark canvas bags. They are terrified because they can't breathe, and they run in fear as it's the only thing they know to do. He sees them and tells Helen to be still and stay with him as the horses will run around instead of over them, but she panics and starts to run away through the tall wheat towards the woods in the distance. He yells for her to stop, but she doesn't hear, and the field has gotten bigger and never seems to end as she keeps running. The horses pass him, but he watches in horror as they come upon Helen and quickly trample her. He screams and runs to her; tears begin to blur his vision and panic stifles his breath. Before she dies, she looks at him in confused sadness, as if she doesn't recognize him, says she is sorry, and then closes her eyes forever. He clutches her to his face, but he is unable to kiss her. He's wearing a mask, too, and he struggles to remove it but can't. It's a gas mask, and he chokes and screams inside of it as the field fills with a deathly fog. The horses have continued running toward the tree line when gun fire erupts from the dark wood. They crash to the ground and writhe in death throes as machine guns open up from every direction.

1

Men crawl out of the dead horses' bellies and continue on toward the forest. They are masked soldiers just like him so he runs to join them as they all disappear into the tangled growth.

Suddenly he is in a trench with seven other men. They are identical, but he knows they are his men, his squad, and they fire their machine guns, but instead of bullets, a bright beam of light blazes forth and makes the enemies put down their weapons, turn around and walk back home. He can see the backs of hundreds of men in dark grey uniforms just walking away like nothing happened. When he turns around, and to tell his men this, they are all gone, and he is left alone. He stands up out of the trench and looks in all directions, but no one is there. The land is grey, torn, and deathly quiet. An icy wind begins to blow. He walks down a dirt road that seems to go on forever. The sky is dark and purple, and the silhouettes of dead trees desperately reaching are the only things that break the barren landscape. A column of soldiers is approaching, and, as they pass him, he sees that people he knows are marching with them, family, friends, but no one looks at or recognizes him as they pass and continue over the hill. It's as if he didn't exist, and he is puzzled by this.

He sees a baseball on the ground and stoops to pick it up, and when he stands again he's back in more recent times at the city park where he's worked so many years. He knows it's his park, though it looks different, and he doesn't recognize anyone until he gets to a monument. Sitting on a bench and looking up at the war monument is his old friend Ernie, whom he'd met during the war. Ernie's still young and handsome like he was then, and now he sits and writes and doesn't see the man (who is now an old man) approach him. Next to Ernie, leaning against the bench is a shot gun. He sits down next to the gun, and Ernie says, "'Bout time you got here. I was ready to leave without you." He doesn't know what that means. Just then a pigeon flies above them as both watch. It dives and turns and finally lands on the statue of the soldier atop the stone pedestal. They gaze in wonder at the bird which they know to be the last of its kind. As it flies away, Ernie takes his gun, aims carefully, and blows it out of the sky. "Why did you do that?" the old man asks, horrified. "Nothing lasts forever," his friend explains.

A young boy in the park finds and picks up the remains of the dead bird. He wordlessly cries and walks away. The old man sees this and tries to run to the boy to console him, but he can't move. He recognizes this boy, but the boy doesn't see the old man. "Tommy!" he calls in his sleep.

Then the old man awakes...

2

Part One

...You see them on the high-way,
You meet them down the pike,
In olive drab and khaki
Are soldiers on the hike;
And as the column passes,
The word goes down the line,
Good morning Mister Zip-Zip-Zip,
You're surely looking fine...

From *Good Morning Mister Zip-Zip-Zip* (1918), Robert Lloyd & Henry Hutt, publisher Leo Feist.

1

He was just everywhere. You'd see him walking all over town. I'd known him all my life, since as far back as I could remember, maybe three or four years old. My parents would take me to the park just down the street from where we lived, kitty-corner from his house, and there he'd be, out mowing or raking or fixing something, or helping some child who'd fallen or couldn't reach that first step on the Jungle Gym or slide.

He spent a lot of time cleaning and maintaining the old war memorial at the park, too. It was the kind that just about every town has, a big limestone base with a bronze statue, now green with time, of a soldier with a soup bowl helmet and a bayonet rifle in his hands. The pigeons loved to perch on it and mess all over the patient sentry. Below on more green plaques were the names of all the local men who'd died. It was one of those things that you'd always seen and didn't really think much about but seemed like ancient history of a time long forgotten. The kids would try to climb it sometimes and sit on the soldier's shoulders or maybe hang some underwear or something from the bayonet as a prank. He'd get real mad and chase them with a rake. The cannon next to it was shiny from all the kids climbing and sitting on it. He didn't mind them. He always made sure flowers were planted around the monument. Poppies came back every year like blazing phoenixes. I'd never seen so many poppies.

"Old Dan the Walkin' Man," that's what we called him. When he wasn't working at the park, he was walking all over town, to church, to the store, to a friend's house, who knew? He didn't own a car or a bike and probably couldn't use them anyway. When he walked, he hunched over and shook a bit, and his long bald head bobbed and rolled like a bowling pin. He was everywhere. You'd turn around somewhere, coming out of a shop or movie theatre or coming home in a car, and there he'd be, out walking to or from someplace. Like the shadow on the ground that follows a cloud in the sky, he was always around, and it was just normal to see him.

One time back in the Sixties, he told me, someone spray painted *Fuck War* on the monument. He left it there for a while, even though he was supposed to remove it right away. He pretended to try, and all the moms were shocked at it and didn't want their kids to see it. But most of the kids couldn't read it anyway, and, if they could, they didn't care. It didn't seem to bother him either, but he finally got it off. Later a rock appeared in the flower bed with the words, 'Pray for peace' carved on it. That's still there. He raised the flag at sunrise and lowered it at sunset. That was his job, taking care of the park.

When I got hit on the head by a baseball, once, he was the first thing I saw when I came to. I hadn't seen him before it happened, but there he was, his big head in shadow hovering over me against the bright blue sky, "You OK, son? Son, you OK?" He called all the guys 'son,' didn't say much to women. It seemed like something always needed fixing or someone helping at Pigeon Hill Park, and he took real good care of things.

Everyone in town knew him or of him, but no one really knew how old he was, though he was always old for as long as I could remember. Yet not old in a decrepit way, but more in a timeless, familiar way, and when you're a kid, everyone seems old, right? Some said he was only in his seventies, others said his eighties. Whatever he was, he didn't seem to change much, almost like he was locked in time and place. He was an evasive old Methuselah, though. I asked him one time how old he was, and he looked at me like he'd never thought of it before. He paused, looked at the sky with a cockeyed glance and said, "Ya know, I don't think Mother ever told me." Then he picked up a handful of dirt from the ground, observed it carefully, blew on it and let it scatter to the wind. "Yep," he said with a smile. "*That* old." He always was kind of strange and vague that way. He reminded me of my grandfather, who had died when I was only eight, cordial, helpful, but never letting you get too close and always slightly quirky.

4

Dan lived alone but never seemed lonely, and his energy was boundless. He said the park was his wife and its children, his, too. It was his family. Some thought he was simple, but I knew otherwise. He wasn't simple, just plain. And more complex than I ever imagined.

As I got older, Old Dan was still around. He looked pretty much the same, but he'd retired from working at the park, and he didn't get out much anymore. He'd had a stroke and couldn't walk as much as he used to. Now, he'd slowly leave the confines of his home next to the park, sit in his ratty old lawn chair, and pull some weeds, or maybe watch the families come and go as he wistfully smoked his pipe, his thumbs under the suspender straps that held up his baggy, two-sizes-too-big trousers that he'd worn for the last thirty years, probably. I always liked the smell of his pipe, sweet, crisp, and lazy. It could fill the whole neighborhood with happy memories.

I was living in an apartment in town by now and volunteered for a social services group that took care of the home-bound elderly, and Dan was in my charge. He still cooked for himself, if you could call it cooking, but I'd stop by with meals or to help with chores and just check on him. He loved his bacon, eggs and coffee. About the only thing he'd make anymore was toast and coffee, so I'd do my best to get as much healthy, colorful stuff inside him. His kitchen always had that great combination of simple smells of toast and coffee that made you just want to sit for a while.

Over time we got to talking a lot and I learned things about him and the town and events I never knew before, like the time the Cubs played an exhibition game at the park. That was back in the '20s, I think. Dan said he got to play, and he even knocked one over the fence. And the time Kennedy came to town, but he wasn't President yet, and Dan got to shake his hand and even got a ride back home in "the young man's" convertible as he made his way out of town. And even how many miles Dan had walked in his lifetime. He figured it was roughly 191,736. How he came to that precise figure, I have no idea, but that's almost eight times around the world!

He also told me why the park, and even the neighborhood was called "Pigeon Hill." He said it was because people used to raise pigeons here, either for eating or racing. This was years ago, when the dumb, slow birds were eaten, while the smart, fast ones got to race. No one does that anymore, here, and the only pigeons around are the ones that sit on the war monument and make a mess. But Dan doesn't mind. He says they remind him of people he once knew and loved. (Sometimes, a dog or cat might remind me of someone, but never a pigeon!)

5

One morning, I brought him his paper from the front porch, and we sat and had some coffee and the doughnuts I usually brought with me. He liked his coffee strong and black, "just like my father," he'd say and laugh, as he was as white as they come, and I'd usually have to dilute mine as he still used an old percolator pot on the stovetop since at least 1930, probably. He liked me to read him some of the more interesting news stories, as his eyesight was failing and he refused to get glasses. He especially liked to hear the sports and the obituaries. It bothered him that some of the older people who were dying in town now, he didn't even know, and he used to know just about everyone in town. All his friends were dead, he said, except for me and the new friends he made every day. "I've worn out my welcome, son. Time to move on," he'd say. "Do ya s'pose God forgot about me?" I'd just smile and shake my head. I didn't know what to say.

One article I read to him was about the last surviving World War One veteran who had just died. *Last Doughboy Laid to Rest* the caption stated. As I started to read aloud, "What's that you say?" Dan asked, as he was almost deaf as a post as well. "Slow down, and talk louder!" he grumped impatiently. So I did, knowing the whole neighborhood could now hear me yelling at Dan, hoping that I wouldn't be suspected of elder abuse.

"Ya don't have ta yell, son, I'm not deaf," he chided.

"Sure, Dan, anything you say," I mumbled under my breath. I could tell that he was extremely taken by the story that I was reading, and he became more animated as he absorbed every word. His white, shaggy eyebrows rose and sank upon his wrinkled brow like billowing clouds before the storm. His tired eyes seemed to dance and sparkle. His gnarly hands began to fidget, and his worn-out walking shoes began to tap a lively march. When I'd finished, I looked at him to see what all the fuss was about. "Isn't that somethin'" was all he finally said. He sure could bluff.

Then I said how sad it was, the passing of a last war hero, and how "old soldiers never die, they just fade away," and every other corny cliché I could think of relating to war since I didn't know a damn thing about it, but I thought would be appropriate. I told him I had a great-grandfather who died in the First World War. He was a hero, from what I was told. Then I realized that I had no idea if Dan had ever fought in a war, since I'd never asked him before, and Dan wasn't inclined to offer much unless he was asked, so I asked. He didn't answer me at first, so I asked again. Thinking for a minute and reflecting, he quietly confessed, "Old soldiers do die. I died a long time ago," as he gazed out the dirty

6

kitchen windows to the park beyond. I didn't understand, and as I was about to say something, he slowly got up and walked to his bedroom. "Are you OK, Dan?" I asked, not knowing what was going on.

"Just a bit deaf," he muttered, so I followed him and watched him open his closet door and try to reach the top shelf. "Give me a hand, will ya?" he asked pointing to a small canvas bag in the far corner behind some boxes. "Watch the traps," he cautioned me just as I was about to touch one with my outstretched fingers.

SNAP! "Awwww!" I yelled in pain.

"I warned ya," he said wryly.

"Not soon enough," I complained, nursing my sore fingers. (The mice were grateful, though.)

"I like to keep my valuables safe from man and beast," he bragged. "Musette bag," he clarified as we walked back to the kitchen table. "There's the ice box if ya need it," he offered generously, so I went to get a cube for my hand.

He slowly took the contents out of the old canvas bag and carefully spread them out on the sticky table without saying a word; like Silas Marner perusing his life savings, he almost went into a trance. There was a tiny diary, some patches, pens, and pins, a VFW card and a few ancient photos, as well as a small bundle of yellowed letters and some tarnished coins. This was history coming to life right before my eyes, and I had to break the silence.

"Sweeet," was all I could think of saying, wondering what all this meant. Dan scowled and cleared his throat. I suddenly felt like Eppie in the coal-hole. "Well, now's as good a time as any," he announced. "Might as well come clean. You're prob'ly lookin' at the last survivin' vet from the Great War... that's the war you just read about," he said, looking at me askance to make sure I understood what he was talking about. "Just an old devil dog that can't seem ta break the chains a life," he said kind of sadly. Whoa! I never knew Dan was *that* old, but that would make him over a hundred. "A hundred and ten," he added, reading my mind. I bet he was an awesome poker player. "Aging's like watchin' paint dry," he said matter of factly. "It takes forever, but once it's done ya think ya could've put a bit more here or there." He sure was a wise old guy. Then, drinking our coffee and dipping our doughnuts, he began his story.

"I never planned on joinin' up; it just happened. It was love; love started it," he confirmed like he'd just thought of it.

I had to smile at the idea that love caused old Dan to fight in a war.

"I had fallen in love with my next-door neighbor. Only she wasn't just my next-door neighbor. She was my teacher. Only she wasn't just my teacher. She was…ahem… married," he said rather sheepishly.

My eyes started to bug.

"Now don't start thinkin' I was some kinda low-life home wrecker," he defended. "I wasn't! I loved her long before she ever became the aforementioned. And I know *she* loved *me*. Problem was, I was five years younger. How could I compete? But that all changed when I was around the age of…sixteen. I was big and mature for my age, and she was still a sweet, wispy thing, all of twenty-one. Aaah, Helen—Helen of Troy! What man wouldn't have fought and died for her? With hair the color of fiery prairie grass on a bright autumn's day, all siennas, ambers and golds—and eyes as big and dark and deep as…as…that first cup of coffee after a long sleepless night."

Yeah, I could relate. She sounded like my girlfriend, Melanie. And I'd never known Dan to be so eloquent.

"Now, this was all back in my hometown of Racine, Wisconsin, you know. No, I guess you wouldn't. Anyway, boys were tough back then, and you had to grow up fast. Not like the spoiled sissies most folks are raisin' nowdays—can't do a damn thing for themselves, always whinin', talkin' on the phone…shees."

Present company excluded, I hoped. As he was starting to drift, I nudged him back to the topic, as I'd done so many times before.

"How did you meet Helen?"

"We grew up together. She and my sister Addie were best gals. Her name was Adelaide, but we called her Addie for short. I'd tag along a lot, when I wasn't banished for all the teasin' I gave 'em. I think I always loved Helen, and Addie knew it. She teased me back and said Helen loved me. I knew that wasn't true at the time, but things changed. We'd all go swimmin' together down at the city beach. Lake Michigan was heaven in the summer, cool and clear like a big ocean. Only it was fresh, not salty. I'd sail in my little boat, or fish from the pier. Sometimes I'd bury Helen and Addie under the sand 'til only their heads and feet showed and then tickled them 'til they screamed. They broke out of the caked sand like demon mummies and threw me into the lake. I liked to tickle Helen's feet. She had the prettiest feet of any mummy.

They'd flirt with the older boys, of course, but it made me jealous when Helen did it.

"I took her for a ride in my boat, once, all by ourselves, and I imagined I was a merchant captain and she was my new bride and I was takin' her to all the ports around the Great Lakes just to show her off. We'd sell our goods and get rich and then sail away to our own little island where I'd built a log mansion. Then a gust of wind caught me off guard, and we flipped over and both took a dive. She wasn't too happy but she got over it. That was the end of my dream for that day.

"Sometimes I'd pretend that I wasn't payin' any attention at all to her, or my chums would want to go and do somethin', but I would make some excuse so I could stay behind and watch her from the corner of my eye as she and Addie did what girls do. Then I caught her lookin' at me, too, and I turned and knew I musta been as red as a port-side beacon because I looked back and she was laughin' with Addie, not in a mean way but in a kind, knowin' way.

"Once, Addie hadn't seen Helen in days, so I asked her how Helen was doin', and Addie looked at me in that big sister way and said she was sick. I said I was sorry but tried not to look too concerned. I didn't want to give it all away, but I did ask her if there was anything I could do or take to 'er, from Addie. She gave me a box of candy and a Get Well card that we both signed. I had to see 'er, but her father greeted me and took our gifts and said thanks, slammin' the door in my face. I sat on the curb across the street, hopin' she might show but she didn't. I knew she would if she could.

"Another time I came in from playin' ball with my chums, and she and Addie were cryin' on the front porch. They were readin' the paper, so I asked them what was wrong and they told me. They said a suffragette from England killed herself by walkin' in front of the king's racehorse durin' a race. She was trampled to death. I didn't know what a suffragette was, and they told me it was a woman who wanted the right to vote. I said that women seemed a lot more sensible than men and that they should vote. Helen put her arm around me and kissed me on my head and said I was sweet. I thought about that woman that got run over by the horses later that night, and it made me sad and afraid, so I got up and woke Addie to tell her to please not do anything as dangerous as that and to tell Helen the same thing. I'd rather have them alive than votin'. She said it was all right and to go back to bed. I didn't like horses for a long while after that.

"Helen eventually went off to Normal School, over in Beloit, to become a teacher, and I only got to see her on holidays and summers.

That was better than nothin'. It was lonely in town without her, and I'd stop by her home or walk down her street just hopin' that she might appear but she didn't. I kept in touch by sending her letters and pictures and poems. Addie let me put them with her letters. Helen and me got to be real close. Then she sent me a letter sayin' she was comin' back home—to teach at my high school.

"When she became my teacher, I'd never looked so forward to goin' to school each day. I was never sick. Sometimes I did real well; sometimes I did badly, dependin' on how much I could concentrate from lookin' at her all day. I'd always try to make up excuses to stay after and ask questions. She was usually more than happy to help me, and sometimes she had questions for me, like what I wanted to do with my life and what my passions were. She knew most of that stuff about me already, but we liked talkin' about it anyway. The bad part was that she lived next door to me. She was stayin' in a room that the school rented for single teachers. That made it that much harder. Now I could see her all the time if I wanted. But she was away more and more on her free time to see her friends...and men.

"When I heard Helen was to be married, I was heartbroken, but I was happy, too, as long as she was happy. We all got to go to the weddin,' as Addie was her bridesmaid. That was the first time I got to kiss Helen. I started to aim for her cheek, but she turned and kissed me clean on the lips and gave me a big hug. Her husband didn't seem very happy about that. He always held her near like she was a pet or a doll or something. We danced, too. I'd never held her that close before, and she seemed like a fragile flower in my arms. Her beautiful hair glowed, and her full red lips were callin' me. I wanted to hold her tight but pretended I was just bein' a good Joe and givin' her a fun turn. Her husband watched every move we made like a jealous snake.

"They ended up buyin' the home she was stayin' in at a real good deal, as a weddin' gift from the school, which couldn't afford it, anyway. But now that she was married, she couldn't teach anymore. That was the rule. Doesn't make much sense, does it? When her husband went to work at the lumber mill each day—he was the supervisor there—she just stayed home and took care of things. She pretended she was happy, but I knew better. She stopped at the school more and more to see old friends, and made sure to see me, too, and asked if I needed any help. I always did. Well, between school and livin' next door to each other, it was just too much of a temptation. Her husband, Lloyd, was a cold, mean bastard, and she'd only married him out of duty. He was a widower and chair of the school board, ya see. I

10

went to see her one Saturday when Lloyd was out with the boys, doing God knows what, when I couldn't hold it back anymore. 'Helen,' I announced, 'I've always loved you and I always will.' I went to pick a flower from her garden. As I handed it to her, I noticed a scratch on her wrist, then a bruise on her forearm, then hand marks on her upper arm as I gently rolled back her modest dress sleeve. 'I'll kill him,' I vowed. Helen began to cry and held me tightly in her battered arms. I cried, too, but I tried to hide it. Before we knew it, we were kissin', from the garden to the porch to the bedroom. It just all happened so fast that we didn't think twice. Lloyd caught us there. He pulled out a gun, but I kicked it out of his hand. He just stood there, smilin' with his bad teeth and a dazed look, when I belted him good, and he hit his head on the dresser before hittin' the floor. The only thing he said before passin' out was 'Dumb kid.'

"Helen and I didn't know what to do. We were both afraid, and we had to just get somewhere and think and talk, so we ran out the back of her house and cut through the wheat fields that bordered it, to make our way down to the harbor. In the middle of the field, it was all quiet and green and still, nothing but the breeze to disturb us, and she pulled me back and made me stop. We caught our breath, and she said, 'Thank you,' and kissed me, and I pulled her down in the tall grass and we made love, all breathless and hot and afraid, but now we knew we could never go back. When we reached the harbor, we climbed into the cabin of an abandoned schooner and we made plans. She would go back to her parents, who had moved to Waukesha, and I would go to Chicago and stay with Addie 'til things cooled down. Addie was in the city now, goin' to secretarial school and stayin' with friends. She was even tryin' to do some actin' on the stage, and I knew she'd understand. My parents would've kicked me outta the house or worse, and my reputation in town was destroyed, anyway, once Lloyd started talkin'. And he'd start talkin', no doubt. I knew Helen would be fine, for now. We just had to sit tight 'til things cooled down."

Dan stopped and rubbed his forehead and looked down at the floor. I could see that this wasn't easy for him. Dan's memory was remarkable for his age, too, since he usually couldn't remember what he ate for dinner last night. Yet now he could remember every detail of what happened over ninety years ago. I must admit that the mushy stuff made me sort of uncomfortable coming from someone as grandfatherly as old Dan. A month before I would have thought that the most interesting thing that ever happened to him was when the toilets backed up at the Little League championships and he had to single-handedly fix the

11

plumbing *and* direct traffic, at the same time.   He'd been cool and focused under pressure that day, and I had never been so impressed.

"I've said enough for now. I think I want to rest some," he said, and so I let him be.

3

On my way home I thought about Dan and World War I. He'd piqued my interest, and I remembered my fascination with war as a child. Like most kids, I'd seen a lot of war movies growing up. Most were pretty lame, though some I liked. My dad didn't like any of them. He'd served in Vietnam but never talked much about it. He thought most war movies were a load of crap, trying to make you feel either really good or really bad about it. "There's good and bad in war just like people," he'd say. I especially liked the ones in black and white. Somehow they made the story more real, like looking into a lighted room through an old pane of glass. The ones in glaring Technicolor just seemed fake, with the bright red blood that you knew was ketchup or colored water.

My favorite of the old black and whites was *All Quiet on the Western Front.* I'd read the book in school, but the movie really brought it to life. It seemed like it was the most authentic with the whole spectrum of emotions, from the highest frenzy of patriotism, like when the old schoolmaster motivates his class to fight for the "Father Land," to the deepest, darkest moments of fear and chaos depicted in the trenches, the hundreds of soldiers going over the top and charging and charging and jumping and jumping at the enemy with fixed bayonets, plunging them into our hearts as we watched. It made me dizzy. Then, as homage, all the dead soldiers were seen marching off into eternity at the end, noble, young, happy, like they were before the horrors of war. It almost made me cry. No Hollywood sap or sentimentalism there.

Sergeant York was just the opposite, with grizzled Gary Cooper trying to portray the part of an "ah, shucks" backwoods boy just doin' right and savin' others as he went turkey shootin' at the Germans. When someone got shot, he looked like a dainty ballerina pirouetting in slow motion with a hand clasped to his chest. The movie just gave me that bad aftertaste you get from too much candy washed down with a diet cola, but I understand the time it was made in, just prior to our involvement in the Second World War. Dan called this war "the sequel" or The Great War Part Two. He said instead of the First World War being the "War to End All Wars," it was really the "War To *Start* All Wars," and he said it very sadly. He was right when you think about it.

The later movies of later wars usually had some dopey old-guy actors trying to pass as young recruits or handsome heroes with greasy hair, big ears, and cigarettes dangling out of their mouths even when they talked. For some reason, the hot, young babes, and there were always hot, young babes in these movies, would always fall in love with these old geezers who smoked too much. Yeah, right. Always tough, always smoking, always talking tough right 'til the end when everyone got killed and the hero walked away with the hot babe. Somehow, I didn't think it was that way when Dan was fighting. How many did *he* kill?

My knowledge of the First World War was pretty vague, too. It was just some faceless war stuck between Abe Lincoln and Adolf Hitler, wasn't it? I knew it started with some duke getting shot. Excuse me, *archduke*. Oh yes, and his wife the archduchess, I guess, was there, too. What kind of way is that to start a war? And the pictures of him in some crazy rooster helmet, with a million medals hanging from his gaudy get-up with epaulets, and billboard sashes, and saber-toothed sword dragging, and long boots up to his crotch, they all seemed like eons ago or a people from another planet or some Walt Disney cartoon. Did they clank overflowing tankards when they toasted, too?

All the officers at that time with their big, stiff collars, riding boots, poofy pant legs, and walking sticks made it all look so proper and civil. This wasn't war; this was a frolic in the countryside. Let the boys be boys. It'll be over before Santa cleans the chimney. I say old chap, isn't it about tea time?

4

I eagerly returned later that day. I was afraid that if I waited too long Dan might not be around to finish his story. He was the oldest and, by far, the strangest man I'd ever known, but there was something very comforting and familiar about him, almost like wearing someone else's shoes and finding that they were as comfortable as your own. I couldn't put my finger on it, but I supposed it was the fact that I had known him all my life. I must have. He was always around.

Dan was puttering about in the kitchen looking for something, so I asked if I could help him find whatever it was.

"Sure—as soon as I remember. Shees..." He was something.

"So, when did you join the army?" I asked.

"Marines," he corrected emphatically, to make sure I never forgot. "I saw a recruitin' poster on State Street, in Chicago. It had a beautiful woman on it dressed in uniform. A lot of the recruitin' stuff back then had beautiful women on it. Sex sold. It sold me, and she reminded me of Helen. It said something like, *"If you want to fight—Join the Marines."* Hell, yeah, I wanted to fight! I was young and angry and foolish. I wanted to fight everybody and everything. I wanted to fight Lloyd and fight for Helen's love. I wanted to fight my family and neighbors who would never understand, and I needed to fight to stay alive because I didn't have any money.

"Addie was my angel. She'd taken me in and took care of me and understood what I'd done but wasn't sure this was the best way of doin' it. I even cooked and took care of the flat she shared with friends while they all worked. They thought I was great. One night after dinner they all got down on their knees and proposed to me. It was a joke, of course, and I said, 'Sorry, ladies, I'm already taken.' We all had a good laugh. Addie took me to the theatre once, where she was rehearsin' for a show. It was one of those old vaudeville palaces, where twenty different acts gave you your money's worth. She would sing a little song and do a little dance, sometimes recite a poem, all stuff you'd never see today. But she told me, she said, 'You know, whatever happens to you, don't fret. Your time will come and your act will out. You just have to wait in the wings, like I do, 'til your time comes. Then, you'll know it's your turn to shine.'

"I guess I knew what she was talkin' about. I knew I'd have to fight for respect if I was ever going to go home and take Helen as my wife someday. I knew my time would come, and I didn't give a damn about some stupid war across the world. But I knew it was the best thing for me to do at the time, so I joined. I lied about my age, of course, but I was big and tough, and they took me. They needed bodies like a bonfire needs wood, to fuel their war machine. I knew Helen wouldn't be happy, but I'd return soon enough, a responsible man ready for the challenges of life."

Was this the boastful tale of an old soldier, or the confessions of a young man, long stifled and hidden? The more I heard, the more I felt that Dan had stored this for too long and really needed to get it out. He looked cleansed, relieved, almost boyish, like he'd been born again.

And I was his father-confessor.

5

"We headed south by train, through Tennessee, Georgia, toward South Carolina, all young men, fresh from the turnip patch. It wasn't so much that we were goin' to war, as much as we were, well, sort of absorbed into it. Everybody was goin', and you just got sucked up into the frenzy like a giant sponge. Remember, this was the war to end all wars, and the world really believed it. We were gonna clean-up and come home smellin' fine after our high adventure and patriotic endeavors. That's what they said it was, "The Great Adventure." I'd never been to the South before. It was beautiful country, but I was shocked by the poverty I saw, and the racism. Mind you, we had racism in my hometown, too, but this was downright antebellum, right outta some story book, real *Dark-Town Strutter* stuff. Got to see some of the battlefields from the last Great War, the Civil War, and talked to some of the old veterans, just like you're doin' with me. I guess we looked at that war like you look at the Second World War now. Shees, I'm older than I thought. Who remembers anymore? I do, and now, so will you. That's better than no one, isn't it?

"I was with a good bunch of fellows on the way down, mostly Chicago boys, and we all enjoyed the trip and the company as we made our way to Port Royal... and Paris Island. Now the real vacation began. This was our trainin' camp, our home away from home. It was like goin' to some big, Boy Scout jamboree. Hah! Paris Island, Paris France, what the hell did we know or care? It sounded like some beautiful resort, with warm, gentle breezes and quaint Southern charm and hospitality. Perhaps we'd be sippin' mint juleps by the ocean while the colored help polished our boots and brass?

"No way. Let's just call it, a *taste* of hell. We arrived late at night, tired, disoriented—*naïve*. It was a dark, strange place, not what I expected, with eerie sounds and bad smells. Maybe we got lost and just stopped for the night? When I realized I wasn't dreamin', we hiked two, maybe four miles, I couldn't tell, always hearin' odd rustlin' in the brush, the strange drone of insects, and the occasional glow of animal eyes watchin' every move we made. I could swear I heard crazy laughter and someone scream in pain. It scared the hell outta me, and I wondered if we'd been shipped to some remote island for the mentally deranged.

"We finally arrived at some cold, old, drafty hall, like a big barn, had a bad supper, if you could call it that, and then tried to sleep. Sleep? Hell, I thought I'd lost my mind. What was I gettin' myself into?

Didn't know I'd be spendin' over three months in that God-forsaken place. Felt like Alcatraz, hot as hell durin' the day, and cold and clammy at night. Most mornin's I'd wake up soakin' wet…and it wasn't always because I was thinkin' of Helen," he said with a wink. We both laughed. "How's your girlfriend, by the way? Melissa, isn't it?"

"Melanie—she's fine. Have you met?" I hadn't ever mentioned her to Dan.

"No, but I hear things. I think she's perfect for ya. Oughta grab her while ya can, ya know, life is short." Short? Wasn't he just complaining to me how life drags on? But he was right. My God, he was like a fly on the wall.

"Well, you just don't know how *good* ya have it 'til you've gone through somethin' like that. They told us 'Forget who you are and who you wanna be. You're Marines now.' I wasn't really sure who or what I'd be, so that was fine with me, but if we weren't droppin' from the heat, we were dyin' from food poisonin'. Ptomaine, ya know—canned salmon and such." I suddenly felt queasy, remembering the salmon salad I had for lunch. "It got so bad we all wondered if Uncle Sam was maybe weedin' out the weak on purpose, before we went to fight. Maybe; who knows?

"The food was lousy more than not, not like the all-you-can-eat buffets they have nowdays. Have you been to that new one out by the shoppin' mall? My God, you might as well break out the pig trough. How can people eat so much?" By 'new,' he meant the one that had been there for ten years. His mind was starting to wander again.

"So was there anything good about this Paris Island?" I asked.

"Sure, it wasn't all heat stroke and diarrhea. We had fellowship and camaraderie and games, and fights, too." His eyes seemed to widen a little and his hands clenched. "When we got on each other's nerves, which was oftener than not, we settled it with a fight, clean and legal. I had my share of scrapes, ya know; they were a lot of fun.

"One typical blazin' hot day—this was summer in the South— 1917—I was bustin' my butt, haulin' lumber or diggin' fence posts or somethin'. We were always workin' hard; we had to. We were building a U.S. Marine camp outta a coastal wasteland, fer chrissake. They'd tried to grow crops there, but that was a failure, so now the corn, scrub, vermin, and snakes were on the retreat! Well, all of a sudden, I didn't feel right. I knew it was the food again, and I had to make a quick exit or I was gonna mess my pants. I'd just washed my only pair of undershorts, just the one pair they gave us; that's how bad it was! I was gonna try to make it to the pier…"

18

"The *pier*?"

"Sure, that was our can, and the ocean was our sewer. Never liked it much. Always afraid some shark might jump up and take a piece a my ass. Well, the Sarge was in a foul mood that day, and he wouldn't let me go. Said it wasn't *time* yet. Besides, I had thwarted his advances."

"Advances?" This wasn't like any war story I'd ever heard!

"He took a likin' to me, well, more than a likin'. Kept visitin' me in my tent at night, bringin' candy and cookies for all the great work I'd done and tellin' me how wonderful I was and what a natural leader I was and how he'd promote me if I did well and all that. He came a bit too close one time, touchin' my hand with mischief in his longin' eyes, and I told him in no uncertain terms that I wasn't interested. Of course, he didn't like that, and after that, he made things hard for me. Nowdays they call it *Don't ask or tell,* but then it was just *Pretend you like women anyway.* Not that there were many fairies in the service—I only knew a few, but they were good fighters nonetheless, clean, mannered, not like so many of the fools and troublemakers we had who'd steal the hat off your head. I didn't ask; I didn't wanna know and I didn't care. Hell, I could spot one a mile away, anyhow..." Dan was drifting again.

"So what happened with the Sergeant?"

"Like I told ya, he wouldn't relieve me of my duties, so I told him that if he didn't let me go, double time, I'd be relieving myself anyway right there. I went runnin' behind the nearest tent and did my business. Then he said I'd be reprimanded for disobeying, so I said, 'How about we fight to settle this instead?' Of course by now everyone within earshot was listenin' and watchin' us, so he says, 'Fine.' I think he wanted to teach me a lesson. Besides, how could he turn me down? I'd heard stories of how he'd almost killed some other boys, just to show how tough he was.

"So there we were—Ol' Leatherneck and Kid Glove Softy squared off against each other that evening. It was quite a spectacle, and the whole outfit was there. He'd worked me hard that day to make sure I was beat for the fight. Maybe he had doubts? By this time I was real lean, not an ounce of fat on my bones, from working long hours in the hot sun every day. My muscles were carved and toned like a piece a ironwood. I was as brown as a coffee bean, too—so brown I was almost *black*! Look at me now, white and blotchy as curdled milk—shees. Don't get old, son. It ain't what it's cracked upta be. (Sure, Dan, I'll defy the laws of nature. Why not?)

"OK, OK, so when the bell rang, I began to have some doubts, too, and he hit me hard, low in the belly, and then came up in my face. I went down so fast, I didn't know what hit me. I saw him hoverin' over me, gloatin' with a big smile on his face. 'Dumb kid,' he said. But then I realized, he was all slow and steady and controlled—but I wasn't. Now I was mad as hell. I got up and started bouncin' all over. The next time he hit, I ducked and hit him hard under the ribs, then I moved to the side. He jabbed at my gut, and I got him fast in the face. For every move he made, I moved faster and surprised him. For every hit I got, I gave him two more. I zipped all over the place. The crowd started chantin,' 'Zip, zip, hit 'im, Zip! Zip, zip, git 'im!' They were all for me!

"At the end of the fifth round, he lunged at me in desperation and pinned me against the ropes with a death grip around my neck as he hammered my face. I managed to flip him over the top, right into the crowd as everyone cheered. They called it a draw, if you can imagine that, but I was carried away…a hero. Diggin' ditches for the next week wasn't fun, but I made my mark. Then he made me Squad Leader. 'Scuse me, son, I need to use the pier."

Part Two

…Good morning, Mister Zip-Zip-Zip,
With your hair cut just as short as mine,
Good morning, Mister Zip-Zip-Zip,
You're surely looking fine!
Ashes to ashes, and dust to dust,
If the Camels don't get you,
The Fatimas must,
Good morning, Mr. Zip-Zip-Zip,
With your hair cut just as short as,
your hair cut just as short as,
your hair cut just as short as mine.

From *Good Morning Mr. Zip-Zip-Zip* (1918), Robert Lloyd & Henry Hutt, publisher Leo Feist.

Dan told me how he used to spend hours on Paris Island Sundays and evenings just playing cards, listening to records, and writing letters, mostly to Helen and Addie. He wrote his parents explaining what he did and how much he'd always loved Helen. His parents responded with a lecture on how irresponsible he was and what a tramp she was. But Helen wrote often, and that's how Dan found out she was pregnant with his child. He called the baby his 'little trick' and told her they must get married as soon as possible. Her and Addie's letters sustained him when very little else could. But his free time was short, and it was back to hard labor, military drilling, and more drilling. The heat was unbearable, and good drinking water was scarce. Some days fifteen or twenty boys would drop, sometimes just waiting in line for chow. Dan said he had to become part camel or wither away to dust.

I could tell he hadn't talked about this stuff in a long time, maybe ever, and I was flattered that he took me into his confidence. He even showed me some of his old records from those days and played me a few tunes on his record player. It was even older than the kind my parents have. The records were 78s and thick and brittle. I dropped one by mistake, and it broke in pieces. I was mortified, but Dan looked at it and said it was OK because he never liked that song that much, anyway. I think it was one about coming back home to a sweetheart after the war.

The songs were fast, jazzy tunes, mostly, real scratchy, usually with some guy singing high and nasally, like he was holding his nose and had been drinking coffee all day. I was surprised at how most of the war songs sounded so peppy, so happy and snappy, like war was one big laugh riot and you couldn't wait to get there. I recognized one, called "Over There," but some were downright loopy like "Good Morning Mr. Zip-Zip-Zip." Dan really liked that one, and I asked him what it meant. He said Mr. Zip referred to servicemen looking all the same, nothing special, uniform, generic, just men on a mission, clones on the march, and all with the same haircut. Another line of the song went "If the Camels don't get you, the Fatimas must." I asked him if that referred to desert fighters who encountered Muslims, or Virgin Mary worshippers, or big hairy animals that spit. He laughed and said they were cigarettes, and everyone smoked them. Duh, Joe Camel. I asked, so apparently, the cigarettes would kill you before the war did? He smiled and said that's about it. My God, even then they were marketing smokes packaged in patriotic platitudes as men marched off to their deaths whistling a happy tune.

When we played the oldies, I could see Dan bobbing around on his cane like he wanted to dance. I asked him if he danced much in the Marines and he said sure but usually with guys so they could practice for their leaves when they would dance with the soft, smiling women that smelled good and didn't step on your feet. He smiled and put his hands out to me as if to show me some short, choppy steps. We danced a little to "Shine On Harvest Moon." I bowed and said, Thank you, sir. He said, Don't mention it, honey. He was a funny old man.

"So what else happened on this mysterious island? You didn't run into Gilligan or any mad scientists, didja?" I joked. He looked at me like I was from another planet. I don't think he'd ever had a television, but he did listen to the radio a lot.

"No, but there was a wild man—half naked, crazy and filthy. No one knew where he came from; he was prob'ly there long before we ever were. We called him Crusoe, as he was livin' like a castaway hermit. Only a few would ever catch a glimpse of 'im as he melted into the brush, like that Bigfoot creature ya hear about. I think he was the one I heard screamin' that first night. My squad was ordered out to get 'im;…yeah, like *that* was gonna be easy. Trouble was, we didn't have any guns—but *he did*. We hadn't had the trainin' yet; besides, they figured a bunch a strong young men could handle one old lunatic. Shees, he darn near killed us all.

"We figured the only way we were gonna take 'im was to ambush 'im. We found his hideaway, just a bunch of scrap wood and brush, and we hid 'til he returned. It was dark when he came, and he could sense somethin' wasn't jake. He fired a few shots, but we jumped 'im, and it took a man to hold each limb while he squirmed and screamed like a hellion. We got 'im cuffed and roped and hauled back to camp, all hung like a trophy deer and no worse for the wear. I kinda felt sorry for 'im and wished we hadn't got 'im after that. They prob'ly locked 'im in the loony bin and threw away the key. But I did my job. They were happy with me."

"Were you rewarded?" I asked, impressed once again with this man of action. When would he become a general?

"Are you kiddin'? We just got more drillin' and more marchin', mile after mile. Recruits were comin' in so fast, they didn't know where to put 'em. Then there were the inoculations, one after the other for every goddam disease known to man—and a few we never heard of. My arm was killin' me so much, I could hardly move it, but we had to move, all the time, move, move, move, parades, and inspections and drills and more parades, with never enough food or water, and when we did eat, boys were droppin' dead from it. I got so hungry at times, I couldn't think straight. I think ol' Crusoe must have been a Marine who just couldn't take it anymore."

Dan looked exhausted as he stared out the window. "I wanna take a nap now," he said, rubbing his whiskered eyes with his big, nubby hands.

Hearing Dan's story made me feel like I'd known him long before I ever did. He was comfortable and easy, like a pair of well-worn walkin' shoes, or an old relative you hadn't seen in a long time but finally got around to chatting with. These days, he did more napping than walking, so I left him to sleep and returned the next day.

"Where ya been?" he asked. "I got a lot more to tell ya." He seemed to forget that I had a life, too. I'd been telling my girlfriend, Melanie, a lot about what he'd been telling me. She really wanted to meet him. I told her that he seemed to know her already, but she couldn't remember meeting him. "At my age I could be dead already and not even know it," he continued crabbily.

He told me how some millionaire ex-congressman from Detroit talked to the recruits on Paris Island, some kind of pep talk on how wonderful they all were and how sacrifice was the only way to become as rich and as wonderful as he was, and that this was their destiny and they were doing their duty for God and country and that because of them there would be no wars from now on; this was it, this was the last war, ever, period, fini. He forgot to mention that he inherited all his wealth and never went a day without the best food that didn't poison him. Oh, and he never went to war, either.

Well, the day grew hotter, and this guy's face grew redder as he blathered on and on, and finally he just keeled over and bashed his head on a chair on the way down. Every doctor they had on the island, which was maybe two, quickly gave him immediate assistance lest he perish from lack of luxury. They had to carry him away on a stretcher. Some pep talk. When he returned to Detroit, he became even wealthier as a major stockholder for auto manufacturing.

(Years later, his grandson, who was the CEO of a large Detroit auto company, had the audacity to fly to Washington, D.C. in a private jet and then beg Congress for bailout money to help his financially-troubled car manufacturing company that couldn't figure out how to make efficient, affordable cars people wanted to buy. This was the third or fourth time this had happened; go figure. As he left the building, he became overwhelmed by car exhaust, fell on the Capitol steps and bashed his head. Strangely, no one rushed to his aid.)

Dan said the island didn't have good facilities for all those thousands when they got sick. Dan got the "grippe" one time and the doctor gave him some salts and chased him out of the office, saying, "If you're not dead, don't waste my time!" It was a harsh and lonely place, and Dan counted the days when he might be able to leave. He even looked forward to fighting in the trenches overseas, anything to break the monotony of camp life. Little did he know.

But then he became an instructor for recruits on the rifle range. "I was a damn good shot," he said, "though I lost Sharpshooter by only three points. Got Marksman instead and an extra two dollars a month. I was happy. Helen was happy, too—sent me a box of candy and a cake. Said all was well, and I was glad to hear it. That night, the white, clean light of the moon as it shimmered across the water from the other shore just about killed me. God, I missed her so, Tommy. I wish you could have known her," he emoted. That was the first time he'd ever called me by my real name. It was always "son." Why he wanted me to know her, I didn't know. She sounded great, though.

"I was finally leavin' the island and headin' toward Quantico, Virginia, to complete my trainin'. Whoo, it was good to get off that sand bar, but then I got ta thinkin'. Maybe the hell ya know is better than the hell ya don't know. But it sure was good to see some civilization again and the cheerin' crowds welcomin' us. And it was good to see women. One young lady even grabbed and kissed me—did *she* smell good! I think I can still smell her after all these years... unless?" Dan stopped to smell the French vanilla roast coffee that I'd bought for him. "Nope, that was her. Then the guys pushed me on, but it sure was nice while it lasted.

"I was assigned to the machine gun corps—the infamous 'Suicide Squad.' They were all a bunch of the best fellows anyone could work with— Barrett, Dahl, Love, Whittaker...," He started to look very sad.

"Do you want to talk later?" I asked, seeing that he might need a break. He nodded his head.

Dan and the boys drilled hard at Quantico, even harder than on Paris Island. And it was even hotter. Then, just when he needed it the most, he got a ten-day furlough to Chicago to see Helen, and, of course, Addie. They knew this would be the last time to see each other before he went overseas—maybe returning, maybe not. Addie offered her place to them, but they didn't feel right about it and decided to stay at a modest hotel near the lake. They registered as 'Mr. and Mrs.,' of course, and Dan even made sure they had their rings to wear, to make it all 'right and proper.' He'd won the rings playing craps back at camp. Hey, he figured they were good luck. When he suggested they get married the next day, Helen brushed it off. She said they would when the time was right, and 'til then, she loved Dan as much as a husband, anyway, maybe more.

It could be sweltering hot in the city, even in September, and the hotel room was no better than a sauna sometimes. They decided to spend their evenings on the beach where it was cooler. At least they had a breeze and each other. A carriage ride under the street lamps and a band concert in the distance was all the entertainment they needed. They swam naked under the stars and drank champagne on the shore, eventually falling asleep in each other's arms. They woke to find a policeman prodding them to see if all was well. It was.

Before leaving for Europe, the Marines paraded in Washington, DC, before President Wilson and cheering throngs. The atmosphere was intense and inspiring, and Dan was awestruck at seeing the Capitol for the first time, all decked out with flags and buntings between the many pillars and columns. He felt like a Roman warrior about to march off to France and conquer the barbarians. He led his machine gun company as Gun Captain, and he was never prouder. If only Helen could have been there. Maybe now, he could return home someday and return to the life he had always wanted. Maybe this was his destiny, to be a war hero. On that bright, shimmering day of a thousand possibilities, how could it be otherwise?

"It was late September, and, finally, we were packin' for France. Finally, I was gonna fight. 'Bout time, I thought, and I was ready; we were more than ready. Before we left, they sent me into town to buy tobacco for the boys. We all smoked or chewed in those days, and the prospect of no tobacco on the battlefield would have been a dismal defeat for us before a bullet was even fired. It was strange, though. The people I met in the streets and shops that day were very different from the jubilant crowds I'd witnessed just days earlier at the parade. They were distant to me and avoided eye contact and spoke as little as possible. What changed? The street sweeper outside was still cleanin' up the mess and streamers from the big parade. The owner of the place where I got the tobacco was an old man. Old man? Hell, he was a kid compared to me, now. He sat behind the counter while his granddaughter, I think, helped me buy the boxes of supply. She smiled sadly at me and said 'Take care' when we were finished. The old man knew all about it. He was wearin' a GAR pin on his vest. He'd fought in the Civil War for the Grand Army of the Republic. He just winked and nodded at me. He'd been there before. Anyway, I was startin' ta feel a bit self-conscious, from all the looks I was getting', so I looked in a mirror on one of those weight and fortune machines as I passed a store, just to see if somethin' was wrong with my face. Maybe people could see somethin' I couldn't. I paid for my fortune just for fun. It said *Beware;* that's all it said.

"New York harbor looked ominous in the cold mornin' fog when our ship arrived. The city skyline and Lady Liberty seemed to give me that same distant stare I got buyin' tobacco in Washington, DC—so long, been nice knowin' ya, hope ya bought some life insurance. That night, under cover of darkness, our convoy set out for the open seas.

"When I woke the next mornin', we were well out on the Atlantic, and any sight of land was long gone. I was on a sixteen-gun cruiser called the 'Dekalb,' part of a seven-ship convoy. They had a good choir on board, and a jolly bunch of sailors we were, singing into the night to give ourselves cheer..." Dan paused to cough.

"...'til we all started pukin' our guts out from sea sickness. The weather got rougher day by day and one man even went overboard. I'd been a sailor all my life, so I wasn't too bothered, because Lake Michigan can get pretty nasty sometimes. It was a long couple of weeks crossin' the Atlantic. Once, we sighted a sub and were all ready to jump ship, but it disappeared and we never saw it again. I spent many a sleepless night on deck doin' guard duty, gettin' wet and chilled to the bone. I'd have a lot more of that comin'.

"When we came in sight of land, it was like seein' home again—'til we could hear the boom of heavy guns in the distance. Then we knew we were in France. St. Nazaire Harbor was like somethin' in a hazy dream, with big crowds of Frenchies comin' to greet us, all fourteen thousand of us. But the crowd wasn't the jubilant crowd that sent us off in DC. Though they were happy we were there, they looked sad, and the women were all in mournin' for the men they'd lost over the past several years of fightin'. They all looked small and old, and they waved American flags while they wore black, lots of black. Some held pictures of loved ones and pushed them at us as if to say, 'Here, win this for him or him or him.' Many were cryin', 'cept for the children. The children smiled and gave us flowers. One little girl grabbed my leg and wouldn't let go. She'd looked lost, and I gave her some chewin' gum. Then she smiled and it was the sweetest smile I'd ever seen. I moved on and hoped she found her family, if she had a family.

"The people were just worn out, and we were their last hope. There were fruit and candy vendors on the dock hawkin' their goods. German prisoners were there, too, doin' work along the docks. That was the first I'd seen of the enemy, those Germans. We called 'em Fritz or Heinie or Hun as well as any other nasty word you can think of. They were big, dirty chaps, and you could see the despair in their faces as they plodded along haulin' and hoistin'. They were sick of war, too. Did they think that now the war would surely end? Maybe they knew we'd never come back? I don't know. The French would spit on them when they could. Anyway, the Yanks were here. But I wondered if we might be too late."

Dan stopped and looked around at his stuffy home that needed a good cleaning. Outside, the world beckoned. "What are we doin' inside on a day like today? Let's head out."

30

11

Dan lived next to the large city park that he'd work at for so long. He was almost a part of it, just like the trees and the fences and the memories of good times. It had playgrounds, ball diamonds, and an ice rink in winter. I used to play fetch with my dog there. Any time I was playing baseball, hockey or just hanging out, Dan was there doing something. I realized he must have still been working into his nineties and doing his job. Now, he shuffled with a cane outside with me and sat in his favorite lawn chair. It was one of those old aluminum chairs with frayed nylon mesh and a sagging seat, but he loved it. He wore his favorite farmer's cap which advertised DeKalb corn; now I knew that was the name of the ship that had taken him to war so long ago. We sat next to his swayback garage which he never used except for storage since he never drove. It still had the original wooden doors that folded to the sides. Looking over to the park where children played, he sighed and looked troubled. "You OK?" I asked. I asked that a lot, with Dan.

"Yeah, just thinkin' that maybe I should have done things differently." He dipped into his shirt pocket and fumbled with a pipe and tobacco. Pulling a match from behind his ear and striking it with his thumbnail—I'll never figure out how that's done—he quickly lit the bowl. Then, slowly drawing on the piece, he puffed, and a great cloud of fragrant smoke billowed around his head.

"We camped a few miles from St. Nazaire and had our first liberty in France. The wine and women were plentiful," he said dreamily. I almost asked him if he was faithful to Helen, but I knew that was none of my business.

"How were they?" I asked.

"What?"

"The wine and the women."

He pondered a moment: "Warm and dry with an earthy bouquet," he answered, not wanting to elaborate.

"But they didn't last long, and soon we were up in the wee hours of the mornin', hikin' to a train and packed into boxcars like cattle. None of us knew what was ahead for us. Ya know, that's one thing about the war, I'll never forget..."

Did he forget anything?

"...never knowin' anything. I don't think anyone really knew what was goin' on, though many pretended to. Have you ever noticed that 'bout life, son? Everyone pretends they know exactly what's happenin' or gonna happen or should happen, but they don't know squat. They all

31

walk around blindfolded and pretend they have a roadmap in front of their faces, and they laugh if you so much as question the directions as they're headed over the cliff they don't know is there!

"Anyway, we were just tryin' to get our bearin's and brace ourselves for what was to come. I nearly froze sleepin' in that damn boxcar."

He took a big puff and daydreamed.

"Then it was more liberty in Bordeaux, real good times. Maybe we weren't gonna fight after all! Our new camp sheltered some men from a torpedoed boat, the 'Antellies,' and some Finnish and German prisoners who worked nearby. Troops from all over the world were there, like a giant meltin' pot of soldiers, all gathered 'round to warm themselves by the heat of war. I had to do guard duty that night in the nearby village. That's all we ever did—guard duty. Hell, I coulda stayed home in Chicago and done guard duty... at Marshall Field's.

"It was November, now, and cold, and I was tired, hungry and thirsty. I could hear the American boys getting' rowdier on the town. Most were drunk, and some were dancin' on top a cars. They didn't have anything else to do 'cept make trouble. I'd rather been with them, havin' fun, than spend another night on dreary guard duty. I needed somethin' to lift my spirits and warm my blood, and it was just my luck to happen upon a cask of wine in the train yard where I was stationed. It musta been forgotten. Finders keepers, losers weepers, I thought. Some old jars were nearby, not that I needed 'em, really, so I tapped into the keg, and I had a good long drink. Then I heard some rustlin' nearby. A shape moved to my left in the darkness, and I yelled, 'What are you doing here?' Then, *'Good morning...'* That's what we were supposed to say. If it was one of us, he was supposed to say, *'Mr. Zip,Zip,Zip.'* But he didn't. As I started to focus and got closer, I saw it was a young lad, not much older than me, sittin' on the ground with his back against the train wheels, and his head held high and back. Was he dead? I couldn't tell, but I had my gun ready. He had something metallic in his hands. 'Drop it!' I commanded. Then he began to vomit—all over the ground, in his lap, everywhere. As I approached, my fears quickly faded as I saw he was one of us, an American, but a civilian. 'Sorry,' he said, givin' me the slimy hand he'd used to wipe his mouth with. 'I dropped it and how,' he agreed with a big grin across his strong, young face. Turns out, he was another Chicago boy from the sticks, scared as hell and not where he was supposed to be. He said he was on vacation doin' some writin'. Some vacation! Said he was joinin' the Red Cross, too.

'Just wanted to see some... ac-tion,' he said apologetically.

'Well, you're not there yet,' I advised, 'Unless you consider a bunch of drunk Yankees on liberty *where the action is.*'

'It's a divi--*diversion,*' he conceded.

'Hey, what's that ya got there?' I asked, getting a better look at the shiny thing he held in his hand.

'Oh, das, joost ein bugle,' he joked, sounding like a German, as he put the mouthpiece up to his eye like a telescope. 'Won it in a—poker game,' he hiccupped to me. 'Confiscate—con-fis-cated off some Fritz.'

'Nice trophy,' I says. 'Care for a drink?' showing him the cask.

'Why not? My stomach's empty now; I could use a refill.'

I offered him a jar, but he held out his empty bugle. 'If you prefer,' I laughed.

Drinkin' out of a bugle isn't easy. It kept him focused. So as we both chatted and consumed the fine burgundy by the tracks, we noticed our boys in town were gettin' more outta hand, and a woman was screamin' on the main street.

'Don't you think we oughtta do something?' my new friend says.

'Let's have a little fun,' I says, so I get my rifle set near two of the drunkest ones, not from my squad, of course, who I figured were botherin' the woman that was screamin'. Then my friend pulls out the biggest damn pistol I ever seen in my life, 'bout the size of that bugle, and I ask, 'Where the hell didja get *that*?' I didn't think the Red Cross ever used the likes of those.

'I'm good at cards,' he says casually. 'Won it off a colonel,' and he touched his finger to his head and then saluted smartly. Shees. So we both intended to scare hell outta the clowns that were disruptin' my guard duty and maybe look good in our rescue attempt of the fair French maiden in distress. Blastin' out the windows and tires of the car that the troublemakers were rollin' on, we yelled, 'Attack—take cover!' The cowards ran like hell. Meanwhile, they dropped the fair damsel like a sack a potatoes in the street. My new friend and I dusted her off and helped her back to her home, no worse for wear. In the end, he spent the night with her, making sure no more harm came, of course. Hah! Me and him kept in touch for a while after the war, but finally we just fizzled out, 'specially when he traveled the world, huntin', fishin', and became so famous and all. I've read most of his books, too. Damn shame when he blew his brains out, though. I always thought writin' was good for the soul."

My mouth had already dropped. I was trying to assemble words in it, like "You mean—you-that was Ernest Hemingway?" I finally fumbled.

"Sure, that was Ernie," Dan grinned.

"But" (I'd done some reading about Hemingway), "he wasn't even there yet," I argued.

"Huh, tell that to him," Dan mused, and pulling out his lumpy, crack-assed wallet which he'd had since 1953, probably, he showed me a yellowed, dog-eared ace of diamonds from a French deck that he'd kept tucked inside. On it was scrawled Hemingway's Oak Park address, signature, and "I owe you one."

"I keep it fer good luck."

"Holy shit! Do you know how much that could be worth?" I gasped.

"Sure," he said matter-of-factly. "One hell-uv-a-night. Those were the good times." Then he smiled and closed his eyes. I just sat there thinking for some minutes and admiring the card and picturing what Dan had told me. Then I said, "Wow, that's some story. Did you ever see him again?" Dan was sleeping now. Boy, could he nod off fast, just like that! So I left him in his lawn chair to dream, taking care to put his pipe away and sticking the card in his shirt pocket.

I still thought Dan might have gotten his dates wrong about Hemingway, though. But after ninety-odd years, he deserved *some* slack.

34

12

Dan hurt his leg playing football to pass the time that Thanksgiving of 1917. He figured he might as well since there wasn't much else to do. Besides, he won eight dollars betting on the game which his team won 13-0. Then he got to spend the next week in sick bay with a few other tough guys who had been hurt playing ball. His hospital bed was next to another boy who hadn't played in the game. His name was Charles, and he was really bad off with mustard gas poisoning or something. He was weak and skinny and pale, and he told Dan he was from Michigan City, Indiana. Then he started spitting up blood, so they knew it was tuberculosis. Dan spent a lot of time talking and joking with him and trying to make him feel better. They played records and sang songs, and Dan was kind of sorry when he left to go back to guard duty knowing Charles wasn't doing much better. Guard duty: that's about all the Marines ever did. They weren't considered 'ready to fight yet.' It was pretty boring but fairly safe.

Dan hadn't received any letters since arriving in France, either. He wrote letters every day, though, just to stay sane. He was depressed, and December arrived, dull and dreary, and he was sick a lot. To pass the time, he made some furniture for his room out of wood scraps. There wasn't that much else to do, so he decided to make something for Charles, a bird house, because Charles had told Dan how he loved to watch the birds back home in Indiana where he fed and studied them. When Dan went to the hospital to give him his gift, Charles's bed was empty and they told Dan that he'd died that morning. Dan went to the funeral the next day. It was raining like always, and Dan left the birdhouse on Charles's muddy grave with a note that he'd stuck in the hole. He didn't tell me what it said. Meanwhile, the rain poured one day, then snowed the next, and the world outside turned to cold, deep mud. Warm mud was one thing, Dan said, but cold, icy mud sucked the marrow out of your bones. At night, in an area that had been shelled heavily, the moon lit up the pock-holed landscape like some other planet, and water glistened like poisonous mercury in every hole.

By the end of December, he was on the move again to Bassens, near a gunpowder factory. Thousands of Chinese from the French colonies were working there, and soldiers stood guard. It was like something out of the old West when the railroads were being built. The French treated the workers like circus animals, counting and prodding them with whips and sticks. Then it was three, crowded, tedious days on a train to Damblain near the Swiss border, now just forty miles from the trenches. The soldiers were all tired, cold, hungry, and bored. That was the worst part, boredom, bored of waiting, drilling, marching, and waiting...

"I took a bath in a snowstorm. That's how desperate I was to get clean and warm," Dan boasted. "Best bath I ever had—beautiful scenery, big, fluffy flakes, winds howlin'. After bein' in the barely warm water, I hopped out and rolled in the snow. That way I knew I wouldn't be cold when I got dressed again. Bein' a Wisconsin boy, I was used to snow, lots of it, and it made me feel kinda homesick. My skin was all tingly, and I was a new man again. At that moment I was ready to conquer the world..." Dan was now getting excited. "Shit, I just peed myself." I helped him into the house. "I'm fine," he grumped as he went to change in the bedroom. He came out and lay on the sofa in the living room. It was a dirty, beat-up thing with grimy slipcovers and several mangy blankets, but he loved it. "I just broke it in," he'd say. Yeah, fifty years ago. Was he ever going to get to fight? I thought war was about fighting, and Marines were always the first to fight.

"A few days after that bath, I won my first battle," he said, relieved, dry, and comfy.

"You did?" I asked excitedly. Maybe now he was going to get to the good stuff. I'd waited days to hear any mention of trenches and battles and heroism and guts and glory, so I now sat expectantly on the edge of the ottoman. I was ready. This was it!

"Sure," Dan said, "I had a quarrel with Corporal Schindler and knocked him clean out, much to the delight of my comrades. He always was a conceited ass." Then he started to laugh hysterically.

"Don't wet yourself again," I advised sardonically. Then he started a coughing fit and I got concerned, but he recovered and collected his thoughts. "Shees—thought I might laugh myself ta the grave there for a moment. If only. Now where was I?"

In La-La Land.

"Ah...1918. It was a new year, and I was ready to take it on. We got new machine guns, harnesses and carts. A new French model of gun— looked like some crazy laser gun outta some space movie. They called it the 'Hotchkiss,' but we called it the 'Frenchkiss'...Get it?"

Yeah, I got it, and Melanie was great at it.

"We could hear the big guns now, off in the distance. At night, the sky lit up and shook like a summer thunderstorm. Only those weren't rain clouds comin'; those were war clouds. I saw some fighter planes for the first time, and the buzzards weren't far behind. They knew death was near, and things were gettin' bad in camp. We were all fed up with

36

conditions; half the company was drunk and disorderly, and if we had to live like hermits in shit, we might as well be in the trenches givin' the Hun hell. Then, our gas masks arrived along with the horses and mules. Can you believe it, Tommy? Here we were, in a modern war to end all wars, dressed up like bug-eyed spacemen in gas masks and usin' the latest death machines. Yet we couldn't survive without feedin', groomin', waterin', and pickin' up after the same beasts of burden that'd been used for centuries. Even the horses and mules got masks. How crazy is that?"

"Sounds like Roy Rogers meets Buck Rogers," I added, casually.

Dan looked like he wished he'd said that and laughed appreciatively.

"Somethin' like that. Now we were ready. All we needed was the blessin' of the high priest himself, General Pershing, to inspect us and bestow upon us his inspirin' words of wisdom. There we were, all ready, spit an' polished, and waitin' and waitin'. I'd seen a war recruitin'poster before, with a picture of him on it, ridin' valiantly on his steed, and some wispy knights of the crusade followin' along in the background in a ghostly cadence of glory. *Some glory.* He never showed. That's what we were supposed to be on, ya know—a crusade. Everything had religious significance and lofty goals in those days. I guess he must have been crusading somewhere else with his knights that day. We were his bastard children anyways, the Marines. He was the father of the army. He didn't like bastards.

"So we all left and hiked some twenty miles to the trainin' trenches. We still weren't ready to fight! After an all-night watch in the trainin' trenches, we hiked *another* ten miles. We were ready to drop dead before the fightin' ever started! Just when I was beginnin' to wonder if we'd ever see action or just die gettin' there, we had a big night in town, wherever the hell we were—I'd lost track by now—some little bohemian dive, good food, drink, loose women as usual, and who should I run into?"

"Hemingway?" I blurted. Who else?

"No, my old buddy Delbert Kappelhoff from Racine, Wisconsin. My God, it was good to see someone from back home—I coulda died and gone ta heaven. We talked all night!"

I was glad for Dan's reunion, but I was hoping for something a bit more historic and exciting.

"My feet were always sore," Dan moaned out of the blue, looking with disgust as he proceeded to remove his old clodhoppers that he'd worn since 1926, at least. "Soldiers *always* had sore feet."

And smelly ones, too, apparently, as I sat downwind from his holey socks. I nonchalantly moved to the other side of the room, next to the window. "Come on, Dan, when did you get to the front?" I asked, almost out of desperation. I'd enjoyed hearing his story so far, but now I needed to hear the punch line, the pathos, the climax, the agony and the ecstasy. That's what I'd read, seen and heard in every book, movie or song about war since I was a kid. Isn't that what war was all about? Where was the blood and glory?!

"It's comin', young man, just hold yer shorts on. War's kinda like sex—lotsa anticipation leadin' to a quick thrill. Then you just wanna sneak home, quietly, in the wee mornin' hours before your lover wakes an' wants ta keep ya for all eternity. You always leave disappointed, if not completely destroyed." Then he sort of turned on me.

"Ya wanted to hear the whole story, so I'm tellin' ya the way it was. There's a lotta nonsense, boredom, and bullshit before any killin' gets done. Maybe we all have to *earn* the right to die? Sad part is, after all that trainin' and waitin', when zero hour comes, none of us really knows what to do. How can you prepare for a trip ta hell? Let's continue this tomorrow. I'm tired," he said and closed his eyes.

13

Dan was right and I felt like an idiot. I didn't know what he was talking about. I considered myself fortunate to have such a good old friend telling me his life in such detail, almost like the grandfather I never really knew, passing on the tales and traditions. I hated to leave him. Would he be alive the next time I saw him? At 110, every hour for him was like a year for me.

I stopped in after work the next day. I could hear his record player was playing *Good Morning Mr. Zip-Zip-Zip*, but it was skipping: *Your hair cut just as short as—your hair cut just as short as—your hair cut just as short as...* So I turned it off and the song died in a deep bass of slow motion, but I couldn't find him anywhere. Maybe he was dancing again and wanted to find a partner? When I couldn't find him in the house, I went outside, but he was nowhere to be seen. Then I looked out past his hedges to the park beyond and saw a group of kids looking down at one of those playground rides that turn round and round, the kind you spin and jump on and try to hang on to. Dan was sprawled out flat in the middle of it. "Christ," I said and hurdled over the shrubs, sprinting to my surely dead friend. At his age he could never take that kind of centrifugal force. My God, *I* even felt like throwing up on those things. It was slowly spinning as the kids looked on in shock. "He won't get off," one said. Another was crying. I found Dan there, limp, white as a ghost,...and smiling as he looked up at the sky, the trees, and my horrified face.

"I hadn't done that in prob'ly a hundred years," Dan croaked, breathless. "The kiddies were good enough to oblige me....phew... but spun me faster than I'd intended."

I had to laugh. "Jesus, Dan, you scared the hell out of me."

"Better out than in," he consoled. We both staggered to a park bench and caught our breaths. His head was still spinning.

"I feel like I've been drinkin'. So where was I? Oh, how's Melanie by the way? Why don'tcha bring 'er over some time. I know she'd like ta hear this, too."

Melanie? Now he made me feel even worse, and how did he know she wanted to come over anyway? I'd been meaning to bring her but hadn't gotten to it. He must be reading my mind or something. Who was this guy?

"Now, let me see, it was...March of '18. Almost a year since I'd left home and still no fightin'."

I felt like *I* needed a drink. His memory was amazing. He could pick up right where we'd left off, yet he couldn't tell me what he did the day before, and he knew Melanie wanted to come over.

"Ya know what happens when ya get a bunch of young men together for a long time with not much to do? Trouble, that's what ya get. Testosterone is the worst drug. As I said, conditions were bad and morale was worse. Some boys got so drunk and disorderly, I had to tie 'em up and lock 'em in a barn. I was Corporal of the Guard now, and I was ready ta knock heads together. Then we had a fight in the mess hall—food was flyin' everywhere, not that it mattered much since we didn't wanna eat it, anyway. Tables were tipped, chairs were thrown— 'Save your energy for the real fight!' I yelled as someone dumped a pan of dirty water over my head. Now I was hot, steamin' mad. I fired my pistol in the air and dared anyone to move on me or I'd shoot their balls off. Then I made 'em all move like good little boys to the barn where I locked 'em all in. I got bawled out in front of everyone by my sergeant, anyway, as I was supposed to keep order. I thought I was. It turned out our company beat up the 79th Company and Cavalry pretty bad, rumblin' that day. The sarge came in later that night and congratulated me on a job well done…and slipped me a bottle of the good stuff. It was the end of a perfect day.

"This was it. That's what they told us. We were headed for the front. We traveled first class, of course, by boxcar, all the bumps and splinters you could handle. After that joy ride, we had a nice, leisurely stroll through the cozy countryside, fifteen miles of rough terrain with airplanes fightin' overhead. We shot at some. I think one was the Red Baron, but I wasn't sure. Golly, was it invigoratin'. Now we were refreshed and ready to fight. Whooweee!"

Dan was getting a little silly. I knew his head was still rattled from the playground romp, so I suggested we go home and have a bite to eat. He didn't fuss. So this is what *I'd* been waiting for. There, near the town of Mont, Mont-something…there were a lot of towns with Mont in the name) heavy loads were carried, mud was waiting to fall into, and lots of rats were avoided or shot. Some rats made good company when they weren't gnawing on some dead guy's face. It was cold, wet and noisy with air raids during the day and gas attacks at night. Not the kind of gas you get from eating—though there was plenty of that, I'm sure, from the crummy food—but deadly gas bombs that burned your skin and lungs and made you puke your guts out and die if you didn't have a mask on to protect yourself. It clung to the ground like a demonic death fog waiting to suck your life out. Some gases made you kill yourself by

40

irritating the skin so bad you clawed at your flesh until there was nothing left. After six days in the trenches, Dan was out for ten and just glad to be alive and take a bath. I thought it was funny what Dan said, about war being like sex. She was the same old mistress, too, and looking older by the minute, from what I could tell. In fact, she was a spent old hag.

14

That Easter, he was in a village now, five miles from the front. Troops constantly passed through, and it was shelled day and night. He was billeted in a small, overcrowded, crumbling farm house, as usual, and it didn't give him much comfort even though he was away from the firing line momentarily. He was on guard duty that cold, gray, lonely morning, and all he could think about was his last Easter, and Helen, and how things change in such a short time. Why hadn't he heard from her? Had she delivered their child? He was consumed with worry. But in many ways it all seemed like a faraway dream, now. Or was that reality and this the dream? He couldn't tell anymore.

He was on guard duty across from a Catholic church, St. Joan of Arc. It had been damaged from the shelling but still offered an Easter service that morning. As Dan sank lower into his gloom and looked around at all the shattered buildings in the village, he heard music, a choir singing like sweet music from the heavens, coming from St. Joan's across the street. Their song ascended to the top of the church's high, vaulted ceiling, then it drifted through the shards of the large stained glass windows like angels flying through the jagged jaws of broken dreams and prisms of colored pasts. When it reached him, he could almost feel the movement of air as it brushed past his cheek and continued on through the weary village. It gave him pause and an overwhelming sensation of comfort that he hadn't had in a long time. Once again, he wondered if he was dreaming, if he had heard it at all. It didn't seem to belong here; it was too fragile and other-worldly. It was then, between the sharp contrasts of peace and war, that a sudden calm came upon him, and he was thankful that he was there at such a place and time. Like his sister Addie had told him, he knew he had a role to play, however small, and that he and this village and this world at war would once again rise, rebuild and renew the promise of life, just like the God that these faithful worshipped there that Easter morning. At least, he liked to believe that. He was still waiting in the wings.

Dan finished the grilled cheese and tomato sandwiches that I'd made for us, and he seemed satisfied and fully recovered from his wild spin at the park. He sat calmly at the kitchen table and continued.

"The next day we were heavily shelled. The lieutenant, sergeant, and I were walkin' through the woods near the village when the shells landed all around us. Dirt and trees were flyin' everywhere and we needed shelter. The two of them hid behind some trees. I didn't think that was such a good idea considering that trees were gettin' hit, so I did what seemed natural at the moment, and I jumped in a big hole left from a shell blast. I figured the chances of another shell hittin' the exact same spot were slim. I was right. I waited it out and they kept runnin' for cover, first that tree, then that. I got back without a scratch, but they both got banged up some. It just isn't fair, is it? Why didn't God parcel out the brains a bit more evenly? A few were killed and more wounded in that one, but the church got the worst of it. The one where I heard that sweet music the day before—it was obliterated. No windows were left for even the tiniest note to escape. Now, I was mad as a snake without a skin. No matter what happened, I was gonna do whatever I could to defeat that goddamned Fritz...April Fools," he said softly.

I laughed. "Good one, Dan, but it's not even April."

"No," he solemnly said, "that happened on April Fool's Day. It wasn't a joke."

"Oh," I said, feeling like an idiot again.

"The next day my machine gun squad worked in front of our artillery while they bombarded German trenches. Now I knew why we were called the 'Suicide Squad.' We were sandwiched between all the fire. The noise was louder than anything you've ever heard, and the shock waves from the blasts were enough to knock you over if you weren't hangin' on to a gun. A shell from either side would have wiped us out, but I didn't care. I don't think I was even afraid anymore; I just fired like a madman and I knew I must have taken out a few. Now, I wish I hadn't killed anyone—but that's war, isn't it?

"We were back in the trenches soon after. Rained for days— knee deep in mud. When we got gassed, we took shelter in our dugout, twenty feet underground. There were more men than bunks, and we became gophers and bugmen, livin' deep down in the earth as they tried to exterminate us from above. We weren't the only things hidin' deep down, though. Rats and lice and bedbugs were lookin' for safe haven – and food. It was a virtual assault on all fronts... and backs.

"Then, we were on the move again—rest camp near Verdun, then Rosary, then sixty miles on foot to Marinus—some of the most beautiful country I ever saw—always on little sleep and all dead tired. What sleep we got was in every place imaginable, above or below ground. True exhaustion finds comfort anywhere it can. We heard of German victories at Reims and Soissons, and we had orders to leave again. The slaughter continued for the Brits and French, sometimes losing tens of thousands in one battle. It was shockin' but numbin' at the same time. Heavy tolls were the price we paid for the war to end all wars, right?

"We slept in the road that night, waitin', always waitin' for trucks, the camions, to take us, thousands of us, anxious and ready, like a giant river of drowsy men, never really asleep, just lost in that twilight between heaven and hell, day and night, sanity and insanity. We were finally transported all closer to the western front, but still we hadda hike, all day and part of the night to Villers-le-Sec. This was a town of refugees, all exhausted and sleepin' in the road just like we did. I'd never slept in a road before that…"

Dan started to yawn, and I knew he was ready for a nap. I was feeling kind of tired myself. I left him to find a good road of my own.

Part Three

15

Dan remembered that France was like a big garden, except where the war had shot up things. I'd never been to France, so I asked him if he had ever gone back, just to see how beautiful it was during peacetime. He said he hadn't, that it would have been strange, like visiting a pious, sober aunt after you'd seen her at her drunken, whoring worst. I didn't get the analogy, but he seemed to. Besides, a lot of sad memories were there. When he and the boys arrived in the village of Lucy-le-Bocage or Lucy as they called it, they were ready for action. I think they liked calling the towns by their first, informal, feminine names. It gave them comfort. And they sounded like girlfriends. They could sleep in Lucy.

They had passed thousands of refugees on the way there, all fleeing the advance of the Germans. Some carried nothing; others carried whatever they could. They passed old women and old men, old horses and old cows—there wasn't much left—and young widowed girls nursing babies that cried for fathers they never knew and a hunger that couldn't be squelched, not until peace, if they survived. Just the very old and very young because everyone else was fighting or already dead. Some had wagons, some just carts, and some had nothing but the clothes on their backs. All were hopeless, and they shouted for the soldiers to turn back; it was over, they said, *"La guerre est finie!"* Most of the soldiers rode in French camions. They were big, overcrowded trucks with horrible if any suspension. It was a hot, dry day, and the dust rose and billowed as each truck went by, covering the refugees and soldiers with a fine, white powder, like flour shaken over bread dough before baking.

Dan's company didn't get to the camions on time and had to hoof it most of the way to Lucy. When he got there, they expected an attack on

45

the town soon, so he guarded the artillery all night, ready for the big drive. He was billeted in a sprawling, old stone barn, this time with some room, and he sat on the dirt floor one morning reading two-month-old newspapers. That's how fast the news traveled. A letter even arrived from Helen that day. It had been written weeks ago, and it said that her child had been born. It was a boy and they were all right, but life was complicated back home and Lloyd was making things difficult. She wanted to break off the relationship with Dan. It just wouldn't work. Besides, she said, Dan had probably already found some sweet French girl, and she didn't want to burden him with a child that she wasn't sure was his. He was too young to know what he was doing. She said it was for the best.

Dan just about died right there. He looked at the broken window in the barn and the shaft of light breaking through that made all the dust in the air glow like evaporated dreams. And that's all he could see was the dust, just dust floating in an empty space that was now his life and soul. Then his rage kicked in. He had to do something. So he went out to the pasture, took careful aim, pulled the trigger, and shot an old cow. He didn't know what else to do. Besides, they'd cook it that day for dinner. The portable kitchens to feed the soldiers hadn't arrived yet, and they had to fend for themselves. Somehow, they still managed to survive.

"Come on, let's get outta here," Dan said. He wanted me to take him to a forest preserve, some park just up the river from his house. He used to walk there often in the old days, and it was one of his favorite places, with woods and meadows and the river nearby. It was one of my favorite places, too, and I was happy to oblige. He was quieter than usual, though, like something was bothering him.

"You OK?" I asked.

"Yeah, yeah...shees," he mumbled.

Dan had probably walked there a hundred times. He knew every tree, pothole, house and utility pole along the way. I wondered if it bothered him now, to be so captive and watch the world go by, when he had so much freedom before, walking wherever and whenever he pleased.

"Kinda nice, seein' the world from this angle. Always wondered what the rest saw as they zipped by me." I vowed to take him out more often.

We pulled into the preserve parking lot, right above the old archery fields, now grown back to meadow. To our sides were the wooded hills, and in the distance behind the tree line was the meandering river. Dan slowly turned his legs to the side to get out of the car as he positioned his cane for leverage. He didn't like others fussing to help him. As he rose, he started wheezing and looked like he might collapse. I grabbed his arm and asked, "You want to go back, Dan? We can come another time."

He looked at me like I was crazy and said, "Retreat? Hell, we just got here." Then he tottered off down the trail. He knew where he was going. I followed along.

"Phew!" I complained, noticing a bad stench coming from the underbrush. "Probably a dead raccoon."

"You think that's bad," he said, "you should have been there after the battle."

"Where's that?" I asked, contorting my face until we were well past the spot.

"Belleau Wood."

We found a bench to sit on while he told me about that day, "somewhere in France," so long ago.

"It was one of the prettiest spots I'd ever seen, ancient woods, fields, country lanes. Bois de Belleau they called it, just a day's walk east a Paris. All nice and peaceful, right outta some story book. This was early June, and the song of birds, the drone of insects, and the occasional clompin' of hooves or the clatterin' of a wagon was all that disturbed the tranquility before we got there. How could any place so lovely host a war as wretched as this, I remember thinkin'. I'd seen battlefields and no-man's land. This was no no-man's land. The place used to be a huntin' ground for the wealthy, they said. Deer and grouse used to roam the dark forest and sunny grasslands. Man was the only predator—now he would become the prey as well.

"The day before it all started, I saw a flock a pigeons, white doves, soar over the area, like peace messengers on a last mission of hope before headin' back somewhere, somewhere far away from this place. Maybe they knew what was comin'. We didn't know what was ahead of us, nobody did; 'course many pretended to, like always. They didn't wanna look stupid. Maps and communication were patchy at best. Information was lost or misinterpreted. Assumptions were made. What we did know was the enemy was comin' this way and headin' for Paris and we had to stop 'im. We were it. That's all there was to it. We were in the second assault on those woods. The first was a dismal failure and we lost a bunch of fine boys. They hadn't learned much before we were ordered to advance again, at five in the afternoon. It was beautiful that day, warm, sunny, just like today. It reminded me a bein' back home on my uncle's farm in Wisconsin, right around milkin' time. I expected to see the cows comin' over the hill any minute and I could smell a fine dinner cookin'. But it wasn't dinner. It was a barn burnin'.

"The enemy was there, somewhere in front of us, in those woods and hills, hidin'. Trouble was we were on the other side of a vast ocean, an ocean of wheat, with no cover or protection. We had to advance over hundreds a yards of open field and take those woods. Those were the orders and we had to do it. I felt like a blind child must feel when he's told to find something in a strange barn full of rats and snakes, rotten floor boards and rusty nails. Where was the artillery to soften up those woods for us and give us a chance to make it over? They said it was gonna be a surprise, that the woods were empty now. Shit—the enemy knew more than we did. Hundreds of snake eyes watched our every move from deep, dark and tangled nests in those woods.

"Before it began, a reporter from Chicago visited us in our dugout and talked with me and the boys. He asked how we were doin' and if we'd mind if he came along to tell the folks back home how it really was. I said sure, as long as he told 'em we needed some better food. The cans of monkey meat we'd been eatin' were enough ta kill anyone. It was corned beef from South America—horrible stuff. He smiled and said he didn't think it would be too hard. We had a last cigarette or got a last chew, joked a bit, then at our time the sound of whistles went down the line. We went over the top, as they say, left our dugout and began our slow advance across those fields and towards the trees.

"It was so quiet and still, not a bird to be seen or heard. I remember how calm and nonchalant everyone seemed, slowly walkin' in perfect formation, like they'd practiced hundreds of times, even in their sleep, just doin' their job, just doin' what they were told, like takin' a little stroll through the grass back home on a nice summer's day. They were fresh, young lads, mostly college boys, with flushed faces, eager eyes, warm, agile hands on cold guns, all just movin', movin' ahead like they'd done so many times. The green wheat under the bright afternoon sun looked cool and refreshing, like a vast pool that we had to wade through. Spattered throughout the greenness were red poppies. I'd never seen red poppies before. They were beautiful and delicate and fragile, like colored tissue paper, and I wanted to pick one and stick it in my button hole or even on my helmet. They seemed to glow out of the coolness of the grass like markers as we passed. I told my boys about it and went to reach for one.

"I saw the tall grass move in front of me, I think, before I heard anything at all, like it'd been blown by a sudden breeze, but there wasn't any breeze. Then the seed heads began to whip back and forth as bullets tore into the grass all around us, comin' from the trees and hills and the grass and the air, it seemed. Boys all around me started droppin', droppin' like grass on the edge of a scythe, droppin' down into the red poppies below, where red met red and got lost in the green. We hit the ground. We were terrified. We weren't sure what we should do. Then I heard the Sergeant yell, 'For Christ's sake, men—come on! Do you want to live forever?' I remember thinkin' I didn't wanna live forever but another day or two woulda been nice. But we kept movin', all that could.

"The field was nothin' more than a cemetery now and we hadta get outta there fast. I could hear cries of agony under the steady racket of the enemy machine gun fire. Boys with drainin' guts and limbs blowed off

49

littered the fields. I wanted to stop and help, but the call was to keep movin', move forward or stay forever on that field."

Dan paused and swallowed hard before he could continue. "My best…my best pal, Earle, George Earle, got hit…hit next to me…his blood hit me in the face, and I could taste it. When I looked down, his head was gone. I tripped over him and was face down in the grass now. I froze in fear. I was breathing heavily, suffocatin' and terrified, like I was drowned in all that grass, but the grass actually smelled good. It's crazy, but that's what I remember, how good the grass smelled. I wanted to stay there, down and drowned where the grass was green and alive and smelled good, but I knew I couldn't. I don't know if I blacked out for a moment or what, but I had a vision of being in the grass with Helen on that day I left home, just a year earlier but like a century ago and a galaxy away. It was warm and quiet and still and I was breathless and hot and afraid and in love, and for a brief second, I was in heaven again. Then I was breathless, hot and afraid, all right, but now I was in hell. Helen didn't love me anymore and death was all around me.

"'Move!' I yelled to my squad. Maybe I was dreamin', maybe I was already dead; it didn't matter. I didn't care anymore. We ran ahead a distance and dropped down. Then the group in back of us would run ahead and drop down behind us, and so on. We weren't toy soldiers anymore waitin' to be picked off. We weren't thinkin' of anything but gettin' outta that field. For every poppy there was a dead or wounded body, and cries drifted over the field like thick smoke. My squad advanced some more, and I noticed we were missin' one, Barrett, Private Barrett. He was hit and down behind us. I went back ta see. He was hit in the leg and arm from what I could tell, so I dragged him forward on our bellies as he shuffled along as best he could. We had to stay low, real low, as the bullets whizzed over our backs. He told me to keep movin' and let him be, that he could make it on his own and he'd only slow me down. I told him as long as we both moved towards the woods we were fine.

"The rest of the squad was now almost to the woods and I could see that there were some downed trees for cover. That's where we'd try to set up our guns and get our bearin' for attack. Other groups had made it in, and there was yellin' and screamin' as they killed or got killed. Most hadn't made it. I asked Barrett if he was all right, but he didn't answer. He was already dead.

"We soon realized that the enemy was hidden like coiled-up snakes inside rocks and crevices and brush, ready to strike with venomous fire. These were the German machine gun nests, dozens of 'em, and for every one there were two more that covered it. It became apparent that we were pretty badly pinned down, and it was hard to tell just where or what we were shootin' at. Me and Love, my seven-man, would try to penetrate the wood and take out the closest nest that was hittin' us, while the rest would stay to cover us and give some of the boys help as the last waves made it out of the field. I'd been in some dangerous situations before, but this was bad. Between the tangle of the woods and the driftin' smoke everywhere, we were blind men, crawlin' our way through the maze, hopin' to find our enemy by sound of gunfire.

"The shells were fallin' all around us now, and the gun nests were perched above and below in every place imaginable. Some were behind rock slabs the size of buses as our boys found their targets and plunged with savage bayonets. Trees splintered and exploded into matchsticks and rained down on us. We were Indians on the attack and howlin' madmen as we fought hand to hand and steel to steel. Modern warfare be damned, now. It was just kill or get killed, pretty much. I knew we were near a nest, so I told Love to cover me as I tried to take the enemy from behind.   Scramblin' between logs and up between rocks, I got upon 'em and shot a few when I got in and was ready to lunge with my blade when the last two shouted out, 'Kamerad!' They wanted to surrender after all that. By then Love had made it there, grinnin' like a kid in a candy shop, and askin' if we'd take prisoners. Then another nest fired on us and we all hit the ground. One of the Germans we captured was wounded, but the other was just ready to give me mine when I skewered 'im like an olive and shot 'im as well. The first thing I did was to grab his German Maxim, the machine gun that'd been givin' us hell, and start returnin' that hellfire. 'Love,' I called, 'you all right? Did you see that?' But Private Love wasn't there. Love was dead. He'd been blowed to bits by a shell I don't even remember hearin'.

"That night we were called back. Crawlin' out of that place was like crawlin' out of some dark, deep cave. We tried to get the dead and wounded out as best we could, but many would stay, stay and rot for weeks under the warm June sun, among the bright red poppies in the green grass. When it was all over, we had Belleau Wood. After almost a month of killin', we had the woods as well as the towns nearby.

"What was once a haven of life was now a monument to death. The trees were all but gone. Now black, twisted stumps reached to the heavens like maimed claws. Maggots feasted on butchered, bloated bodies. The smell of deadly gas bombs mingled with the stench of decay. The peaceful, invitin' villages of so many centuries were now in ruins. That was it. That's war, Tommy."

51

We got up and slowly walked back to the car. I didn't even notice the smell of the dead raccoon, now.

"Thanks for bringin' me. It sure is a beautiful day," he said as he took a last look around. It was.

Part Four

18

I had dinner that night with my girlfriend, Melanie. We happened to be at the all-you-can-eat buffet restaurant that Dan had disparaged earlier. I don't know how we ended up there, but there we were. She thought it was funny, what Dan had said, and looked around and whispered "Oink, oink." I snorted, and we laughed. I told her about my day with Dan, about the story of his fighting at Belleau Wood in France.

"So when can I finally meet him?" she asked. She'd wanted to come on my visits for a long time. I'd told her a lot about him already. We decided to go the next day as it was Saturday, and we both had the weekend off. "We'd better make it soon. Old doughboys don't live forever," she joked, more serious than not. Melanie was the sweetest person I'd ever known, and Dan had been right when he'd said, "Better grab her while ya can. Life is short." What was I waiting for? She looked just like Helen must have looked the way Dan described her, with her deep, dark eyes, and full, wavy hair that glowed in the sunlight like prairie grass on an autumn day.

Melanie was an English teacher at a junior high school, and she loved to read more than anything, and she tried to pass on her passion for books to her students. Lucky for me, I *wasn't* her student and she *wasn't* married and we *hadn't* known each other since childhood. (We'd met about a year ago at a party.) Sadly, she knew she was witnessing the slow extinction of reading on a daily basis, in her classroom and everywhere else. I had to hear about it all the time. She's predicted we'll be an illiterate nation of imbeciles by the year 2025 with no idea of where we came from and totally clueless as to where we are going. She also believed that the last conventional paper book will be published around 2045. "That will be the year I die," she said.

"No, you won't," I said. "We'll write our own books and live a long, fruitful life." Melanie said the last published book will be placed on display in the Smithsonian. The name of the book will be something like *The Secret to Great Sex While Losing Weight and Getting Rich Quick!* It will be an instant best seller, of course. Museum goers will marvel at how such art was ever conceived. The topic of books would then lead her to talk of a strange and not-so-distant future. It reminded me of one of my dad's old records that I used to listen to called *In the Year 2525,* by Zager and Evans in the '60s. I loved its up-tempo guitar rhythms and haunting verses. It was science fiction put to music, but it rang so true when I first heard it. (Melanie and I have danced a pretty good swing to it before.) Could it really happen? As I got older, I realized it already did. I even played the song for Dan once. He loved it and did his old-man jiggle dance to it. I forgot I left it with him, and the neighbor complained that he played it too loud when I wasn't around. He said it "got his juices flowin'."

Melanie and I sat and ate. The buffet was pretty good. So far I'd seen a woman whose nipples showed through her tee shirt and a biker type with a black eye. Professional eaters in baseball caps surrounded us on all sides. Then a picture came to my mind of spoiled, lazy brats at the buffet, eating, texting, playing video games and listening to their iPods all at the same time while their parents just ate and looked depressed. Not a word was spoken. Then I glanced over across the room, and there they were. My dark vision was reality. Yikes, what an abomination! How could I ever have kids after witnessing that? But then I looked into Melanie's eyes, and that didn't seem so hard, after all.

19

We got to Dan's that morning and brought coffee and doughnuts. I think he would have been disappointed if we hadn't. Besides his old percolator just wasn't cutting it. I'd told him I was bringing Melanie, not that he minded, but I thought I should anyway in case he had anything planned, like maybe walking around in his underwear or something, which he did on occasion. When we went in, we noticed flowers in a jar on the kitchen table. It was a wild arrangement of daylilies, peonies and irises, but it looked pretty good. "That's a first," I said. He'd picked them from his yard.

"I think they're sweet," Melanie purred, propping up the stems that looked droopy. Dan was in the living room, relaxed in his favorite lounge chair, the one that looked like it had been through the war with him, and he acted surprised, like he didn't remember we were coming. Maybe he didn't. "What's that smell—like cinnamon?" I asked.

"Oh, that's just my new bathroom spray. Thought it might be nice to try it."

I introduced the two of them, and they acted like old friends. Melanie was interested in the book that Dan was reading. It looked rather dated, but it still had a paper jacket that his big, pink hands just about covered as he held it in his lap.

"I didn't think you could read anymore," I said noticing on his head the reading glasses that I'd never seen before.

"Oh, well, I can if I really have ta. But I like your readin' aloud better."

"I'm glad you like to read, Mr. Marshall. May I call you Dan?" Melanie chirped.

"Only if you say it as sweet every time," he flirted.

"I love to read, too. What book is it?"

"Oh, just an old war story I haven't read in, prob'ly, eighty years. Talkin' with Tommy here lately made me wanna get back to readin' some a my old stories."

"May I see it? I like old books."

Dan handed over the hardly worn copy with its original paper jacket. It was dark blue with a strange picture of a reposed naked angel lying in front of a weight lifter whose head hung down. I recognized the title immediately. Melanie first looked at it like she'd seen a ghost, then she giggled and gave it a skeptical eye as she asked, "This is incredible, but this must be a reproduction—isn't it?"

No, Dan said, it wasn't. It was a first edition of *A Farewell to Arms*, signed by Hemingway himself with the inscription, "Keep the home fires burning, but not *too* hot."

"Holy...! Do you know what that could be worth?" Melanie bubbled.

Been there, done that, I thought. I filled her in on what Dan had told me before, about meeting Hemingway and their wild adventures.

Dan looked at her and smiled. "You two sure get excitable over old stuff." Then he winked at me as if to say, *See what I mean? You're meant for each other*. "I got a bunch more just gatherin' dry rot there under my bed," he confessed.

Melanie looked at me like she'd just got the Daily Double on *Jeopardy*, won the lotto, maybe found the Holy Grail. "I'd love to see the rest, Dan. Wouldn't you, Tom?" she asked about as calmly as she could when her head was about to explode.

"Sure, I like books." What was I saying? I didn't read as much as I should, and she scolded me all the time for it.

Melanie helped Dan out of his chair like the house was on fire. I thought she might even carry him. Dan didn't seem to mind it, though, when she helped him. He milked it for all its worth and grabbed her tightly.

"Would you mind, Tom?" she asked. I was going to do it anyway. I pulled a battered cardboard box from under the bed and placed it on the mattress. Then I blew the dust off of what were maybe two dozen books, but not just any books. "Oh-my-God..," mumbled Melanie, staring, mouth open. Neatly packed inside the box with their original paper jackets and stacked bound-side-up were just about every classic book of the 20th century. There were Hemingways, of course, four of his, and Fitzgerald's *The Great Gatsby*, Steinbeck's *The Grapes of Wrath* and *Of Mice and Men*, a few by William Faulkner, and Salinger's *The Catcher in the Rye*, Truman and Tennessee, Bradbury and Vonnegut and others, all first editions and all in excellent shape. Some were even signed. Melanie's eyes glazed over like doughnuts, and she started to breathe heavily...

"Do you ha...," she was about to say. "Never mind. May I?" She took the books carefully out and lovingly laid them on the soft bed, touching each one, tenderly, like fragile birds.

"Have they been in this box all these years?" I asked.

"I was gonna give 'em away...," Dan began. (Melanie was about to faint.) "But I decided ta keep 'em. I had 'em on my shelf for years and they were just gettin' dusty. I want you ta have 'em, Tommy."

56

"Me? Wow, Dan, that's awfully generous, but..." Melanie had now come close to me and was hugging my arm and looking wistfully up at me with her big doe eyes, the big, dark doe eyes wherein floated children, our children, children who liked books, and the eyes spelled out c-o-l-l-e-g-e; this could pay for our children's c-o-l-l-e-g-e! She smiled and batted her eyes at me. What could I do?

"Well, thanks, Dan, that's very kind of you," I said. Melanie sighed. After admiring them like ancient works of art, we gingerly returned them to the box and sauntered back to the living room, like happy explorers who'd just raided a pharaoh's tomb.

Part Five

Pack up your troubles in your old kit bag,
And smile, smile, smile!
While you've a Lucifer to light your fag,
Smile, Boys, that's the style.
What's the use of worrying?
It never was worth while.
So, pack up your troubles in your old kit bag,
And smile, smile, smile!

From *Pack up Your Troubles in Your Old Kit Bag and Smile, Smile, Smile* (1915), Felix Powell & George Asaf, publisher Chappel.

20

I got the coffee and doughnuts while Melanie chatted with Dan. When I returned, he was already telling her about the next chapter in the war, without me.

"Don't stop on account of me," I kidded sarcastically.

"No need to. I was just givin' her the background—shees. So, we saved Paris—the *first* time. We all needed a rest, all that was left anyway, and the French threw us a party like no other. We'd driven the Germans back, and they were gonna have a parade to honor us. It was the Fourth of July, warm, sunny, and we all looked like hell—we'd just got back from the fightin'. We got up early, tried to clean up as best we could, and headed over to the parade. Everyone yelled out to us, 'Vive les Marines!' The women grabbed and kissed us, the children threw roses at us, then grabbed and kissed us—it was all too much. It was all women and children and old people who just cried and cheered, and the few men, as so many had died, just cried and saluted and kissed the women and children, thankful to even be alive. The main street, the Champs Elysees, was one giant river of flowers and shouts and tears and smiles. It all ended around noon, and I was glad as I was gettin' kinda tired.

"Then we headed over to this huge munitions factory for lunch. The French had decked it all out in flags and banners and hundreds of tables and thousands of girls. Girls were everywhere; the ones that worked there and elsewhere were all waitin' for us. My God, what a sight! Was I dreamin'? They fought over us, too, and there were prob'ly a hundred to every soldier. This would be our greatest test yet, I thought, as I made my way into the crowd. What was for dinner? I felt like the main course. Each table had American flags at it, and that was where the soldier were supposed to sit, surrounded by beautiful French girls... and a few not so beautiful but nice just the same. There was champagne and wine, good red wine, on each table. I'd never seen so much wine and so many pretty girls. Maybe I'd died and gone ta heaven after all? That was fine with me.

"At the same time everyone was instructed to untie the champagne wires, ya know those little cages on 'em, and slam the bottles down on the table. All at once hundreds of bottles exploded while corks flew high into the air, landing on other tables and heads all around. It sounded like a barrage of cannons, like the factory was goin' up, and everyone got hit with spray, and toasts were made. Dignitaries with lots a dignity spoke in a dignified way. More toasts were made and more backs were slapped and everyone felt important.

"Then there was music, all kinds, even one of our colored units was there, and they were playin' jazz for the first time, and the French were goin' crazy over it. Then a French marchin' band came in where they left off, then the jazz boys came in and followed their lead, and they went back and forth, like some kinda challenge, like artillery volleys back and forth to see who could be the loudest and the best. The crowd went wild! All the girls at my table were askin' me, '*Dancons?*' Did I want to dance later and I said sure, I promised them all. Was *that* a mistake.

"The food came out on big platters at all the tables in several different courses, and by this time we'd all drunk quite a bit already and my head was swimmin'. It was a great feed and the girls kept askin' me if I wanted more, more, and more, and I said no and rubbed my belly and said I was gonna explode, and they thought I meant I was pregnant and laughed at me. Ha, ha—oh my God! After lunch we all danced, and I took turns with as many as I could, but, when I'd try to sit and rest, another would grab me and beg for more. It was all too much. I felt like a celebrity, and, in a way, I guess I was. We all were. We'd saved their city after all. Later, we went back to our camp, put our guns away and headed back to town for an all-night liberty."

Here I thought *I* knew how to party, but after hearing Dan, I was beginning to feel like an old man.

21

"Did you meet anyone *special* by chance?" Melanie asked Dan. She had a unique gift for getting information that I certainly didn't have. She knew about Helen and was hoping that Dan had been able to fall in love again.

"No, no. It was all laughs, ya know," he said in a maudlin kind of way. "I wasn't up ta anything like that. Still thought of Helen...and all those left behind." Melanie reached out and took his hand.

"Dan, what did you mean when you said you 'died a long time ago'?" she asked almost hypnotically.

I'd forgotten that he'd said that, but I must have mentioned it to Melanie. I thought it was just a figure of speech, a metaphor for his sadness, like maybe his heart was left over there with his dead friends or something, but Melanie heard it differently. I started saying, "I think what he meant, Melanie, was..." when Dan cut me off.

"No, she's right, Tommy. I did die—but now it's time for me ta come back ta life." We both looked at him like we expected an alien to appear. Then he looked at me blankly, like he didn't even know what he'd just said, like his soul was somewhere far away in France on a country hillside, long ago, where the blue sky met the green earth and the clouds rolled gently by, giving brief shadows to the land and then moving on so fast that you wouldn't have noticed a flash of dimness if you so much as blinked. That was how the war was in his mind, I thought, a large passing cloud that casts a shadow on every dark detail below. His tired eyes got misty, and then he smiled and his face came back to the present again.

"I've wanted ta tell ya this for a long time, son. But when you've lived a lie as long as I have, it's hard ta give it up." He looked down at the floor like a child about to confess some mischief. "You see, I'm your great-grandfather, Tommy."

"What?" I asked smiling, like it was some kind of a joke. I looked at Melanie who seemed less surprised.

"Yes, you're my great—"

"What are you talking about? My great-grandfather died in World War One. His name was Frank, Frank Loudon," I emphasized in case Dan didn't hear. My God, I thought, Dan's really gone over the deep end. He'd been so rational up until now. What happened? Now Melanie took my hand and gave me a look of moral support.

"I know it's... it's hard to believe," he continued, "and I don't blame ya if ya hate me for it—"

"For what? Hate you for what? That you're a goofy old man and after all this time of telling me your life story, you're under the delusion now that you're part of my family?" I'd never gotten mad at him before, but now I was really upset and I didn't like it.

"Please—My name isn't really Dan Marshall. It's Frank Loudon."

"You're crazy! What else have you made up, huh? I suppose everything you've told me so far is a lie, a fairy tale, some joke. Do you think I'm some dumb kid?"

"Tom, please!" Melanie cried. Dan was teary now and had his hand over his brow. I felt really bad and I didn't want to hurt him, but I felt betrayed. Was he deranged or just full of crap? I had really respected and believed everything he told me. How could I be so naïve?

"Come on, Melanie, we'd better go. Sorry, Dan, I think we all need a break."

"Are you all right?" she asked him.

"I'm fine—It's best we talk later."

We went out to the car. "I think I better tell the agency that Dan needs help. He may need to go in a home," I told her. I wasn't just upset; I was concerned. "He might get hurt," I reasoned.

"Tom, what's wrong with you? I think you're blowing this thing *way* out of proportion. Besides, what if he is a bit silly and made some stuff up? And can you be *sure*, one hundred percent that he isn't who he says he is? What do you really know about your great-grandfather?"

I looked at her like she was crazy now. "Jesus, how..." Then I looked into those big, dark doe eyes of hers, and I thought I started to see some sense, some logic. What difference did it really make, and why was I so upset? Why did I take it so personally? Dan always was sort of strange. But it *was* personal. Was I afraid of confronting my own fears of getting old, or was it something else, long hidden since childhood, a sense that I was connected to Dan in some odd way that I wasn't sure about? Maybe I did always love him like a grandfather or great-grandfather, for that matter. Maybe, I could see something there that was long hidden; I just never realized it until now. But how dare he lie, after all this time! Dammit, I believed him! "I'm going to see if he's OK," I said. She started to come along. "No, you stay here, please. It's all right." When I got in the house, he was still in his chair with his eyes closed. "I'm sorry, Dan (or whoever you are, I thought), are you OK?"

"Yeah, just restin'."

"You want to talk some more?"

"No, not now. Come back tomorrow. I'll still be here." He smiled.

Part Six

...Another little drink,
another little drink,
another little drink wouldn't do us any harm.
Another little drink,
another little drink,
another little drink wouldn't do us any harm.

From *Another Little Drink* (1916), Nat D. Ayer & Clifford Gray, publisher B. Feldman & Co.

22

We drove back to Melanie's. I was in a daze. We'd have to go back tomorrow, I told her. I had to find out what this was all about and, if anything should happen to Dan just now like death, I wouldn't be able to forgive myself. She said that she'd promised to see her mother then and that I could handle it, she was sure. I wasn't. We went up to her apartment and talked and had a drink. "Really, Thomas...," she said. She called me Thomas when she wasn't happy with me or thought I was being childish. "I was shocked at your behavior. You totally overreacted, like totally. It's a miracle the poor man didn't have a cardiac right then." She went to look at her mail. She was right; I was a jerk. But then I explained to her what I'd been thinking about in the car, my acknowledgement to myself that Dan meant more to me than I ever realized and my feelings of betrayal with this sudden confession/revelation of his and that I was subconsciously shocked to hear it. She looked at me like I was from another planet and said too much self-psychoanalyzing wasn't good for me. Plus, I said, I felt guilty for not having treated him better when I was younger.

"Guilt?" she wondered. "What could you have possibly done—or not done—to feel guilty about?"

"Oh, me and the guys used to make fun of old Dan sometimes: hide his tools, impersonate his weird walk, steal his underwear off the clothes line, stuff like that."

"Men, huh! How do you ever get past the age of nine?"

I offered to make our dinner, and she didn't refuse. Then I massaged her shoulders and feet, and now she was feeling better. I'd made up for my sins, and we had some more drinks. We talked some more and laughed, then tried to watch some TV, but that was so lame and annoying we snuggled on her bed and read instead. She only had what I called 'chick' books so she gave me a copy of a book that her students were now reading and would be taking a test on shortly. It was *The Old Man and the Sea* by Ernest Hemingway. I remembered reading it back in school. It was about fishing and nature and guy stuff, and I liked it.

"I'll quiz you on it in the morning," she teased.

"Can I spend the night?"

She looked at me like I was a nine-year-old. "Of course you can, silly. You earned your keep." Then she kissed me real nice, slow and sloppy. After that we didn't get much reading done. We made love and I told her how much I loved her and needed her, and I asked her if she'd marry me. It was as good a time as any. She said she might, if I passed the test.

That night I had the weirdest dream. It was based on the book Melanie gave me that night. In it, Dan was the old man and I was the boy, and we sailed out in a giant old shoe, one of Dan's, which was our boat. We went out to sea further than we should have, but it wasn't the sea; it was more like a time warp.

Dan said, "We'll have to turn back now or we'll never get back, and I don't wanna stay an old man forever. I need some sleep!"

I asked, "Well, what about the fish?"

And he said, "Fish? There's no fish here! We came to catch a glimpse of truth."

I didn't know what he was talking about, and that's when I saw her. She was grasping at a slippery rock out in the water, the water of time. She was a beautiful young woman, but more like a mermaid or siren, and she was calling my name, "Tommy!" I got the impression she was Helen, and she wanted to tell me something. That's when the sharks came and circled all around her, but instead of shark fins they were more like camel humps going faster and faster, spinning the water when music began to play. The song was *Over There*, from the war, but sped up and crazy and skipping, *Over there, over there, over there....* I yelled to Dan, "We've got to save her!"

"Don't worry about her," he grumped. "She's fine. We've gotta get back!"

I couldn't believe it. He was just going to leave her there? When I turned around again to see her, I was amazed to now see the Virgin Mary calmly sitting on the rock and nonchalantly smoking a cigarette. She smiled and waved goodbye to me, blowing a big smoke ring in the air. This is insane, I thought. What does it mean? We were getting closer to the shore and I could see crowds gathered to greet us. Dan looked exhausted, like he might die, and I said, "Please, God, don't let him die yet." I took the boat in to shore, and the crowds started chanting, "Methuselah, Methuselah!"

That's when I woke. Later I told Melanie about it and asked her what she thought it meant. She said it was probably the wine.

23

I visited Dan the next day. I had brought some Danish kringle, made in Racine, as a peace offering and cooked him his favorite bacon and eggs. He was fine and acted like he didn't even remember what happened the day before. He probably didn't.

I asked him, "Dan, if you're really my great-grandfather, please tell me what happened and why you kept it from me, and my family, all these years." I was calm and polite, and he looked surprised that I even brought it up.

He sat quietly and fiddled with his fork. "Have you ever wanted to die?" he asked.

I had to think for a moment. Then I was able to say, "I've felt like dying before but I don't think I ever wanted to die, per se." That was a lie. I got seasick so badly once, I did want to die at that moment. When I broke up with my first *real* girlfriend in high school, I thought I wanted to die. But, then, if we had stayed together, I might not have met Melanie, and she's *way* better than Tiffany ever was. Tiffany was a vegetarian who couldn't dance or sing worth a damn. I think those were the only times.

"Back then I wanted ta die. But at the end I turned into someone else. That had ta do, I guess." He continued. "I felt like a real whore after that night, that night we spent in Paris after the big party they gave us. I thought that maybe the booze and women would make me feel normal again, make me feel happy for a while. But it didn't. I felt empty and alone. I couldn't shake the thought a losin' Helen, the only woman I'd ever loved, and the memory of losin' all those fine, young boys in battle. I couldn't forget all the killin' I did during that month it took ta take those woods. I felt changed, old, dis-attached from life, like nothin' mattered. I was just a soldier, a killer...an animal. I was *Mr. Zippity-Do-Da* but I wasn't lookin' or feelin' fine. I lost count a how many girls I slept with or how much I drank. That night was just a blur like everything else.

"When we got back ta camp early the next mornin', two a my boys from the squad were carryin' me. They said I'd proposed to at least ten girls and they'd all accepted. I'd be busy till I was a hundred, they joked. Ha, ha, hoo, hee, ho. They thought it was hilarious. We all had some breakfast and tried ta sober up some and luckily got the day off ta catch up on things, washin', repairin', and the like. I looked in the mirror and saw Death-warmed-over. I gave myself that same vacant stare I'd gotten back home before shippin' out. I smelled bad and felt like crap. I wished I was back on that field, rottin' away.

"It wasn't long before we were movin' out again for another round a hell. We were goin' for the big drive at Soissons. We were reorganizing at a camp far from the front now. I hadn't been sleepin' well and woke early that morning to relieve myself before the sun was up. It was so quiet and peaceful, cool and dry, that I decided to take a walk and clear my head. A large hill was nearby and the stars were now just beginnin' ta get washed out by the light on the horizon. It was incredibly beautiful, that time between night and day, dark and light. I wished I could stay forever. I slowly climbed and found a rough path that took me between the tall grasses and flowers. The birds then started to sing, and it was like hearin' 'em for the first time, each clear note piercin' the air like angel song. When I got ta the top, it felt like I'd been climbin' for hours, though it was only minutes, and there was a lone rock and one scrubby tree at the top. I sat on the rock and looked out over fields and valleys with the sun just peekin' over the earth and bathin' the world in a soft glow.

"I could see for miles and, yet, as I looked down, it seemed I could see details I wouldn't have noticed otherwise. I could see leaves movin', even their veins, and blades of grass catchin' the glint of dawn, and drops of dew and small insects drinkin' the drops before the sun claimed them ta the sky once again, and, as the sunlight hit each drop, it broke into a million colored rainbows and it was blindin'. I thought I must be dreamin' and rubbed my eyes, but it was all still there as plain as day. I suddenly felt the highest elation and deepest sorrow at the same time, and I broke down and cried. I cried like I'd never cried before, like I was just born and like I just died. I cried because it was all so beautiful and I was there to see it, and I cried because it was all so terrible and so many I'd known and loved would never see it again. I cried because I couldn't understand how God could have such wonders and such horrors coexist at the same time and so close. Would this be destroyed, too?

"Then I had a vision of the future, of things to come. I saw columns of soldiers passin' down below in front of me through the mornin' haze, but it wasn't during this war, it was in another to come. I saw angry, hateful people who thought that this war would bring peace and prosperity for generations, return home disillusioned, and spread more anger and hate around the world. I saw starvin' children beggin' in the streets, and sick women sellin' their bodies and souls for meager food and the warmth of another body. I saw mangled, faceless men

66

return home to empty lives and empty promises. And in the Kaiser's eyes I saw the glint of a future leader for Germany, with the same angry eyes and baptized by the fires of this war, who would go out later and destroy more than anyone could possibly imagine. I was horrified, and I now wept with fear."

Dan sighed deeply and put his hand over his eyes. I took his other big hand in mine and said that it was all right, that he didn't have to talk anymore. His hand felt weak and fragile like a soggy sponge.

"I'm fine, Tommy. I want to talk. I need to."

Part Seven

...Oh! Oh! Oh! It's a lovely war,
Who wouldn't be a soldier eh?
Oh! It's a shame to take the pay.
As soon as 'reveille' has gone
We feel just as heavy as lead,
But we never get up till the sergeant brings
Our breakfast up to bed...

From *Oh! It's A Lovely War* (1917), J.P. Long & Maurice Scott, publisher unknown.

24

"We marched all night. All night it rained, and the night went on forever. That night we marched to the battle at Soissons. It was an eternal night of eternal rain, just puttin' one foot in front of the other, of endless mud, and the splash and suck of each step took a bit more of your life away as you moved from the blackness toward the blackness. We were sleepwalkers, walkin' through an endless wet nightmare as every step got heavier with every drop on every pound of saturated gear. Soon we'd go down, down to the muddy center of the earth, and there at last we'd find our peace.

"When we stopped, it was as if the earth had stopped turnin', but the rain continued as we all slumped over to the side of the road. I, like many, was too tired to even remove my pack, and I slept dead on the side of the wet road under the drippin' trees. The patter of every drop on my helmet burned a hole into my numb brain. Then, as dawn tried to break through the water, the gray dimness seemed to call us all from the dead, as each soldier slowly woke and stared and wondered. Where were we? The French were with us, and portable kitchens across the road beckoned us all like frozen moths ta flames, so we all moved to the light and heat of the fires. It was good to feel the heat, and we were given coffee and chow. We only slept 'til noon that day, after marchin' all night, but it was enough to refresh me, and as the day drew on, it cleared and warmed and the memory of that previous night slowly dried up like the puddles on the ground all around us.

"We were near a chateau, and I could hear band music in the distance. The sky was bright and clear now, and I made my way toward the music as the sun shone warmly on me and felt so good. I entered a path that led me to a boulevard of trees on either side of the path, like soldiers standing guard. This led me to several terraces of stone steps that brought me down into a sunken garden with old, mossy statues and up the other side where I could now see where the music came from. It was a magical place, a place I would have loved as a child.

"Below on a lawn was a French band practicin'. It looked like somethin' from a Sunday picnic, and it was hard to believe this was real when German artillery could be heard in the distance. Others had heard the music, too, and gathered to hear the cheerful tunes. The conductor acknowledged us, us Marines, and the band began to play "America." I sang along but could only remember the first verse, "My country 'tis of thee, sweet land of liberty, of thee I sing. Land where my fathers died, land of the pilgrims' pride, from every mountain side let freedom..." *BOOM!* A shell tore through the air and landed right in back of the band. We were on the hillside near the trees and had a little cover, but sheet music and brass instruments flew in all directions. The Germans didn't like that song very much, I guess; they gave us a friendly reminder that war was still on. I carried whoever was still alive back to the chateau with some other boys, then we headed back to camp, and the fun was over.

"The sky quickly darkened again and rain came. We were all lined up to wait for trucks, more French camions to take us closer to the front. We drove all night packed in tight, like cigarettes. We didn't get wet this time but we couldn't move, and every rut and jostle evened you out and made you smaller.

"When we stopped it was dawn, damp and sticky, and we crawled out of the trucks like arthritic old men crawlin' outta bed and allowed to flex our joints. Climbin' over a fence, we hiked a mile or so over farmland with our gear 'til we got to a large hill. It was more like a small mountain, really, covered with trees and brush, and we had to carry all our gear to the top, where, we were told, we could pitch camp and rest. The hill was swarmin' with divisions from all over the world, doing what we were doing and talkin' in strange languages and dialects and milling about like different colored ants around an anthill. The horses whinnied in protest and slipped and staggered up with heavy loads, tearin' the ground with desperate hooves. This took most a the day, and when we got our camp set, I was just about ready to catch some shut-eye when our company was told to go down the mountain again, across the field, ta bring up more supplies. When we arrived, no one and nothin' was there. So we waited. When nothin' still arrived, we went back, across the field and up the mountain again.

"By now it was gettin' dark and a storm was blowin' in. As we scrambled up the steep gravelly face, it began to rain, then it began to pour. As we slipped and slided and crawled our way to the top, a bolt a lightnin' come outta the dark sky above my squad and split a tree clean in half. I could see everything as bright as day, for a split second, and then it was black. The tree musta been a hundred feet high, but I could feel the electricity hit my helmet and run down my body to my boots where it blew out the ends of 'em. My toes were now exposed as they smoked, and I couldn't hear anythin' but a loud, thin ringin' in my ears. When I touched my helmet, it was hot as the huge tree came crashing down all around us. None of my boys were hurt, but a few others were dead underneath the massive trunk shards, and a few more injured. A horse was crushed. We left the dead and helped those injured slowly up the dark, wet mountain.

"When we got to the top, all was chaos with everyone runnin' around tryin' to find their things and their units and bumpin' into each other in the dark. My hearin' was slowly comin' back, but it was like a blind, deaf nightmare where you're lost and no one understands who anyone is or what they're doin' and you try to talk but nothin' comes out and no one hears you anyway if you could. My squad tried to stay together, but we gradually got lost in the shuffle as everyone was gettin' ready to move out. Bugles blew, men yelled, and horses cried, but all I could hear was geese. It sounded like a flock a hundreds a geese when they took off from the river near my uncle's farm. I couldn't find my company and now I couldn't find my boys. Everyone was yellin' at the same time, but no one was hearin'. Men and horses were runnin' in all directions tryin' to get packed up when I saw one, a horse, bolt outta the darkness past a last smolderin' fire on the ground. It musta spooked before it went runnin' through the embers, kickin' sparks and logs. I could see the glint of terror in its eyes as it charged through the dark mass of men and beasts. It went racin' right at me but I jumped to the side. When I got up, the horse had been reined in, but a group was gathered 'round next to it, looking down. The horse had trampled a soldier to death.

"I finally got pushed in line with the nearest group and figured I'd catch up with the rest of 'em later. Nobody seemed to notice as I looked like everyone else who didn't know what was goin' on. We were all goin' the same direction, anyway. Then we all started down the mountain like a giant, slitherin' snake of soldiers goin' somewhere to do somethin' like so often in the past. When we got to the bottom, we joined with others, and the snake kept slitherin' along, gettin' fatter and longer as we went. Then we got to a crossroads and stopped. Two other big snakes were there and we had to figure how we were gonna blend all these snakes together as one. I'd never seen so many soldiers, tanks, trucks, horses, mules and guns all put together before. Hell, this was gonna be some battle.

"So now I got some time to look around a bit as all the brass snakes talked and argued for an hour over which was the best way to do things. I'd been marchin' next to the same soldier ever since we left the mountain, and he kept bumpin' into me and clearin' his throat all the time and spittin' and in general bein' a real pain in the ass, so I thought I'd try to see who he was. It was dark as pitch, and you've never seen such dark 'til you've been lost at war at night, on your way to God-knows-where. There were a few low lights around as the mass tried to meld together, and, as I looked over at the fella next to me, I thought I'd seen a ghost, a ghost of myself when I first joined the Marines and went to Paris Island and got scared ta death. He was a private, a new recruit, prob'ly older than me but as green as the grass is long. Never seen battle, never crapped in the woods before either, no doubt, but he was about as close a likeness to me as I'd ever see. The Germans called 'em doppelgangers, I think. He was a bit heavier, slightly taller. We introduced ourselves. He was from Milwaukee—what a small world. I asked him if he had a girl back home, and he said he did. I asked him her name, and he said Helen. Then I said to ask her how the baby's doin', and he just looked at me funny and then laughed like he got the joke. Poor kid.

"The snake continued on and on and on all through the night 'til dawn. I still hadn't seen my group, but I hoped I would as all my gear was hopefully with them. More likely, it was still back on top of that mountain, left in the confusion. Anyway, we all knew what to do: kill or get killed. That's all you had to do. But my rifle was gone. I'd get another soon enough when the fightin' started. When we stopped, we knew this was it. The great big snake yawned, stretched, broke up and slithered away in every direction. Medusa was on the loose. And soon, many men would turn to stone."

Dan said he wanted a drink of water and had to use the bathroom. I went to get us some water in the kitchen. I heard him shuffle to the bathroom but then heard a thump and a groan. "Dan, are you all right?" I called. "Dan!"

25

I remember calling 911 on Dan's old rotary phone. It was a big black thing on his kitchen wall that had been there so long it was a part of it. I think I just stared at it a second, trying to remember how it worked. Oh yeah, stick finger in hole and dial, duh. My cell was in the car and I felt that every second counted. Three numbers took an eternity.

He'd slumped over in the bathroom and hit his head on the tub going down. But he could talk and was still coherent.

"I couldn't get my, my, you know… zip unstuck," he mumbled.

"Don't talk now; I'm calling for help and you're going to be all right."

"But I wanna, Tommy, before it's too late…" Shit, he wanted to keep talking, even now.

"We'll have plenty of time after they get you to the hospital." (Will we? I wondered.)

I placed a towel under his head and raced to the phone that had been on this wall since Bell invented it. Thank God, it worked. Well, it must have, since I'd used it to call Dan before, but one never knows. The paramedics were stationed just around the corner at the firehouse on the other side of the park and could be there in no time. Please God, I prayed as I sat next to Dan on the bathroom floor, don't take him yet. Just give us a little more time, please. After one hundred and ten years, another day or two wouldn't change the course of history, would it? I took Dan's wrist and checked his pulse. His eyes were closed, and he was quiet. Where was it? I couldn't feel a thing! Damn it, I wish the EMT's would hurry up!

I rode with him in the ambulance to the emergency room. When they asked me my relation to Dan, I stumbled for a minute and had to think. At first I thought neighbor, then friend, no, caretaker. But after knowing Dan all my life, I realized I was more than those, also. I was also a student, admirer, watcher, and wonderer of this crazy, mystifying old man. "Yes?" the nurse asked, wondering if maybe I needed a doctor as well.

Oh, what the hell. "Great-grandson," I casually stated like I'd been doing it all my life.

I called Melanie from the waiting room, and she came right over.

"How is he?" she asked, giving me a comforting hug. I kissed her head.

"Alive. They're running tests."

"Ah, poor baby." We sat, and she took my hand.

"How's your mom?" I asked.

"Oh, still telling me what I should do and complaining about Dad, as always. But she's still Mom and I wouldn't have it any other way." She smiled and put her head on my shoulder.

I thought about my parents and how I needed to see them more. Why hadn't they told me more about my family, I wondered? If Dan was who he said he was, why didn't they know it? We lived practically next door to each other, for Christ's sake. And what was my great-gramma's name again? I'd only heard it a few times in reference to my grampa's upbringing. His father had died when he was very young, and his mother had raised him alone. Damn, what was it? Nancy? No. Nellie? No, close, though. Ellie... that was it. She'd been Great-Gramma Ellie, I'm sure.

"Ellie," I said aloud, thinking to myself.

"What?" Melanie asked.

"That was my great-gramma's name, not Helen."

Then a doctor came out to talk to us. He said Dan was stable and resting now. He'd blacked out, perhaps from a mini-stroke, got a mild concussion when he fell, but other than that, he was lucky to be alive at his "advanced" age. With any luck, he'd be with us another year and be the oldest living resident in the state. Gee, that explained everything. I was waiting for him to tell us the "max" time he'd have to stay here and maybe the "mega" amount of money it "might" cost. But I breathed a sigh of relief.

"Can we see him?" I asked.

"Sure. Family's always good for recovery," he advised. "Just don't get him too excited."

We followed the doctor to the tiny, curtained alcove where a tiny, curtained man was lying peacefully in bed with his eyes closed. The thought came to me that that was just how Dan would look when he was dead, but thankfully *not* now.

"We'll get him a quieter room just as soon as we can," the doctor said. I nodded.

"Hi, Dan. You OK?" I feebly asked. He smiled and nodded back.

"Hi, Dan, it's me, Melanie." Dan opened and closed his big spongy hand, and Melanie took it. "Is there anything you want?"

He motioned for her to come close, and he whispered to her, "Just take care of my boys." She nodded. "Thanks, son," he croaked.

"What are families for?" I replied. We left him to rest, and I walked Melanie back to her car.

"You gonna be all right?" she asked me as she got behind the wheel and shut the door.

"Yeah. I'll stay here tonight, just in case."

"You wanna tell your parents anything—I mean about what Dan said?"

"No, just that he took a fall and I'm here. Thanks for coming."

"What are families for? Call me." We kissed through the open window.

"Oh, by the way, Ellie's short for Helen," she said as she drove away. I cried a little that night, but not with Dan. I didn't want him to see.

26

The hospital released Dan after two days. They said he ate like a horse and was no worse for wear. Plus, if he stayed any longer he'd want to just get up and walk home, anyway. He probably would, too, so I took him home.

"How was it?" I asked, as we drove.

He smiled and nudged me with his elbow. "The nurses were *hot*."

I laughed. "Was the food any good?"

"The *best*."

"Wow, sounds like paradise." I was glad he'd had such a good time.

"Glad to be gittin' back home, though." He sat quietly and watched the traffic zip by. I wondered if he remembered what had happened before he fell and if he wanted to talk anymore.

"We'll talk more when we get home," he said.

I just looked at him. No damage there, apparently.

"Here, turn here!" he blurted.

"What?" I quickly hit the brakes and did as he asked. "What for?"

"I need ta see some old friends." Hmm. He was as mysterious as ever.

"Where we going?" I asked, wondering if he thought "home" was somewhere else.

"You'll see. There, up ahead, on the right." He had me pull into the old veterans' home. I'd never been there before, but I knew about it.

"Have you been here before?" I asked. He seemed to know all about it.

"Been a while, but I've visited." He let me help him out of the car and we made our way in.

The nurses at the front desk lit up when they saw him like they'd seen the return of a lost hero. "Dan! How are you? So good to see you—welcome back." He enjoyed the attention and knew each nurse by name and introduced me as his great-grandson while he chatted and caught up on the news. They were thrilled to meet me but confessed they didn't know Dan had any children.

"I didn't either, up until this week," I sheepishly added. He shuffled down the hallway like he was at home, stopping to shake hands or say hello to the various residents. We got to a small aviary, and he stopped to talk to the birds.

"We put that in a few years ago and it's been his favorite," one of the aides told me.

"Has he been coming here long?" I asked.

"As long as anyone can remember. Betty would know. She's been here the longest. Hey, Betty!" Betty was probably only in her early sixties, but she looked more like seventy. I could tell she worked hard but loved her work and probably wouldn't know what to do when she retired. She said she'd been working there thirty-seven years and Dan had been coming all that time, volunteering to visit at least once a week. She said the nurse she took over for when she started said the same thing. Dan had been coming here every week for over sixty years, since the home was built. He helped do whatever they needed him to do, and the residents were crazy about him. So this was one of those places that he would walk to all those years. It was a good four miles from his home.

I watched him as he talked; he seemed to know everyone. The turnover rate for patients must be pretty high in a place like this, I thought, with most not living more than a few years before passing away.

"Does he know everyone here?" I asked Betty.

"No, Dan hasn't been in for a while, since his stroke. Most in this section are new, I think, since then." He was talking to them like old chums.

"Did you know he was a World War One vet?" I asked her. She just looked at me like she hadn't heard correctly at first.

"No, I didn't," she said vaguely. "The last vet we had from that war died, let's see…, twenty years ago? My."

It always made me sad to visit nursing homes. Melanie's grandfather had Alzheimer's and we'd visited him once. He didn't recognize her, and he was now reduced to a shaking, drooling bundle of bones who could do nothing for himself. I was shocked, and Melanie cried when we left. As I looked around at so many of these men, who were once so strong, independent, and heroic even, I wondered why they had to end up like this. Would I be like this, someday? Dan was one of the lucky ones.

27

When we got back to Dan's place, I made us some sandwiches and coffee, strong, black coffee, "just like his father." And he continued to talk.

"Now where did we leave off?" I reminded him for the first time.

"We were tired and hungry after marchin' all night to the front. We rummaged through the belongin's of the dead already there on the field to find our breakfast. That's all we had. I got my rifle from one; I knew I would. After a brief rest we moved out. I was still with my twin from Milwaukee, and, after asking a few questions of others, I found out that my company was just ahead and was movin' in the same area we were. I knew I'd find them soon. The enemy was on the other side of the hills just in the distance. They'd retreated and knew we were comin', and they were ready. Beside the dead soldiers all around from the previous battle, there were blowed-up trucks and guns and dead horses. I felt the worst for the horses. They couldn't protect themselves. They didn't belong here.

"We'd gotten to the hill where the Germans were. We were on one side and they were on the other, shootin' at us with machine guns and artillery. But, like many times, we'd gotten there sooner than expected and our artillery didn't know it. Now we were getting' hit from both sides, and many of us were being killed by our own guns. We were pinned to the hillside like an insect collection. 'God damn it, what are they doing?' I shouted. We had ta get outta there! Then I heard a familiar voice. 'Loudon, where the fuck have you been?!' It was my sergeant; I was back with my boys. They were behind me the whole time. They'd even carried my gear between 'em.

"By now the shells comin' from our side had moved further ahead, where they shoulda been all along, and now we had a chance to make it over the hill and race down the other side. We got to a low gully and hunkered in with some protection from a brush line and we set up our guns. We were able to hit the bastards pretty well from there and give the rest of our boys some breathin' room to advance. By evenin' we were near a small town, now blowed ta bits. What was once a charming rural village was now a pile of rubble, except for one small flower box still attached to a burned-out shell of a building. The flower box was untouched and full of bloomin' red geraniums. A butterfly was sippin' nectar from one of 'em. Craziest thing I ever saw.

"It'd been a warm day so we were all dyin' a thirst. I found a water pump nearby. I let half my squad go get a drink while me and the rest stayed with the guns. When they hadn't returned in a while, I got concerned and went ta find 'em. When I got there, I found the pump was gone, just a large smokin' hole with dead and maimed bodies all around. Two a mine were dead and two more badly wounded, nearly dead. A cart was nearby, so I piled the live ones on and hauled it back to the road where I knew one of our trucks was set up for medical attention.

"It was gettin' dark now and I went back ta find the rest of my crew. But they were gone, too! Maybe they'd gone to find me and the others? So I went back to the pump, or what was the pump. There, with the rest of the dead, were my boys. They'd been ambushed and lay there...all dead. My God, Tommy, I'd sent them all to their deaths. Without knowin' it, I'd sent them to die..."

Tears began to stream down Dan's face now. I felt I had to say something.

"But you didn't know, Dan. It wasn't your fault. Like you said, 'That's war.' It wasn't your fault."

"No," he said, "I was their leader, I was responsible... and I should have known better. Then something snapped in me. I cracked. All I could think of was what a failure I was, what a waste. I'd lost the only woman I'd ever loved and my child, and now I couldn't even keep my own squad alive. I pulled out my pistol as I knelt beside my dead boys and I held it to my head. I closed my eyes and said a last prayer. I asked God to forgive me. Then I began to squeeze the trigger. But I couldn't do it, I couldn't, Tommy! I couldn't even kill myself. All I could do was fall in a miserable heap and cry on one of my boys. I cried and said how sorry I was and asked them all to forgive me, forgive me for not keepin' 'em alive, and forgive me for losin' 'em in the chaos of that march down the mountain, and forgive me for not dyin' instead of them....

"Then I realized the body I was cryin' on wasn't one of mine. There, in the fadin' light of day, I turned him over. Half his face was gone, but I could see the other half, the half that was me...*with his haircut just as short as mine.* It was the new recruit, the young kid from Milwaukee that I had met in line. It was Dan Marshall. He was clutchin' a pack a Fatimas in his hand. He musta come for a drink and a smoke and got blowed away with the rest of 'em. Shit, I thought...*Ashes to ashes and dust to dust....* What I did next, I don't know why or how or even how long it took, but all I know is I was walkin' back to the road carryin' another wounded in my arms. It was dark now, and I was wearin' his things, Dan Marshall's.

"Shells were landin' all around me but I kept goin' toward the road. Then I felt them. Bullets like hot needles burned into my shoulder. Then I heard the scream of a shell off to my side as it blew and threw us in the air and into the ditch by the road. I was still conscious and felt somethin' warm and wet on my face. I guess I passed out. A vague memory came next, of movin'...like in a bumpy, dark dream...sandwiched between other bodies. I was floatin' on my back. It was hot and dark, and I couldn't breathe. I must be in an ambulance. Red dots passed before my eyes like burnin' poppies. I thought I smelled fresh grass, then the stench of dead, rottin' flesh. I must be dead, I thought, I must be goin' ta hell. I *was* a dumb kid, Tommy, I was just a *dumb kid*." Dan looked down in shame and wiped his eyes with his hanky.

"We're all dumb kids, Dan," I said.

Part Eight

...Don't cry-ee! Don't sigh-ee!
There's a silver lining in the sky-ee
Bon soir, old thing! Cheerio, chin-chin!
Nahpoo! Toodleoo! Goodbye-ee!

From *Goodbye-ee* (1917), R.P Weston & Burt Lee, publisher Francis, Day, Hunter.

28

Melanie stopped over to see us. She was a welcome break, and Dan lit up as usual in her presence. So did I. "Here, I brought you this," she said to him. It was a pager.

"Clip this to your pants or pajamas, and if anything happens and you need help right away, this will page Tom. Just press this button." She clipped it on for him and showed him how it worked. Dan looked a little embarrassed.

"Great idea," I said, "I wish I'd thought of that sooner." Dan motioned me over with his finger and whispered to me.

I translated for him. "He says that he doesn't wear pajamas and it would be hard to clip it anywhere else." Melanie laughed.

"No problem, just keep it on your nightstand and carry it with you to the bathroom." Dan looked relieved.

"Do you feel up to going outside?" I asked him.

"It's a lovely evening," Melanie said. Dan nodded. He clung tightly to her arm as we went out. Sitting out by the paint-peeled garage where we usually sat was a new lawn chair. I'd bought it for him. It was the canvas fold-up kind with arm rests and drink holders. I hoped he'd like it and wouldn't miss his 1965 sway-assed Kmart Special.

"Where's my old chair?" he asked.

"In the garage." I put it there in case he fussed; I didn't have the heart to throw it out—yet.

"There's holes in the arms."

"Those are for drinks." He didn't seem to get the concept or care, so we helped him position himself for landing. He plopped in and said thanks. We sat next to him on a bench and looked over at the park. Families were enjoying the fine evening. Crowds could be heard cheering over at the Little League fields after a crack of the bat. The American flag fluttered gently on its pole and caught a glint of setting sunshine. Dogs barked and sniffed each other. Children fell down and cried. Sweethearts held hands and shared an ice cream cone. Life was good.

"What happened with Ellie after the war?" Melanie asked him out of the blue.

Dan lit his pipe and drew a deep breath through his nose, so as not to inhale the smoke. Then he blew out a slow billowy cloud of sweet smoke high into the air. I liked the smell of that smoke. It circled above us like a dream.

"I never called her Ellie. Others did, but I didn't like it. To me she was always Helen, the most beautiful of all. I knew I had to see her after I got out. They released me from the hospital in Paris after a month. I got off easy. Many there were missin' limbs, eyes, noses. Others got it in the gut and died slowly, some just days before the Armistice. Some had lost most of their face. I felt sorriest for them. The doctors even tried to make partial or full masks for these men, to hide the holes and deformities. You tried not to look horrified when you saw them, but you couldn't help it. They were the phantoms of war. They'd be the walkin' dead. I'd been hit with shrapnel on the side of my face and back and had bullet damage in my shoulder. So my face was intact but looked a mess, scarred and bruised. You can hardly see the scars now for all the blotches and wrinkles. The nerve damage was minimal, but I always shook some after that. Still do. The mental ward was the saddest. Men twitched and shook and cried. They howled like monkeys. Many were lobotomized. Because they remembered.

"Everyone was talkin' 'bout how the war was gonna end soon. It had to. There was no one left ta fight 'cept us Americans. But now I was Daniel Marshall, and Frank Loudon was dead. He'd been killed at the office while havin' a smoke 'round the water cooler with the boys. Happens all the time. It took me a while ta get used to the new name. Every time the nurse or doctor said it, I had ta think. Was I him, or was he me? After a while I couldn't tell. The war was like a bad dream, and, after all, my stat sheet and I.D. said Daniel F. Marshall, but I still felt like someone else. One time someone called out 'Frank!' and I said, 'Yes...? That's my middle name.' F. stood for Frank, so there was still a little part of me left, and that was OK. But how was I gonna approach my family...or Helen? They thought I was dead or would think so soon. I didn't know how fast they'd get the news. I'd sent Addie a letter sayin' I was all right from the hospital. I told her there was a little 'mix-up' at the hospital and I'd be home soon. I didn't want her to worry, in case she'd heard somethin' already. I wasn't sure what to do.

"I'd never have begun this insane charade unless I knew somethin' first, though. Dan Marshall was an orphan. I'd found that out when I first met 'im. His girlfriend would get over him, no doubt. Lots a people disappear durin' war. So I was discharged from the service. I stayed in Paris a few weeks. Even then, I knew I'd never be back, so I wanted to enjoy what I could. I ran into some of the same girls I'd met before, when we were on leave after the parade and during that wonderful lunch. I pretended not to recognize 'em and most stared a second and then looked away. But one sweet girl, Marie, the one I liked the most, immediately hugged and kissed me and said how glad she was that I was still alive. I asked her if she was mad that I'd proposed to her when I was drunk and had no intention of honorin' that act. She laughed and said I was crazy and didn't remember such a thing. She insisted we have lunch and held my hand as we found the nearest café. I told her a little about what happened and she didn't pry or judge. She was just happy to see me. I told her I'd be leavin' soon, to go back home. She looked sad and then invited me up to her apartment for coffee. She lived with her mother. Her father and brother had been killed in the war. We had our coffee together at the kitchen table with her mother, then Marie took my hand and led me to her bedroom. I was embarrassed and asked if we should be there with her mother in the other room, but she just put her finger to her lips and kissed me. Then she told me to lie down and rest. I was tired so I did. Before I knew it, she was naked, on top of me and makin' love. I left while she was asleep and left her a note that said how special she was and that I'd write her. But I never did."

29

"I arrived at New York early on a foggy mornin' just like the first time when I left to go overseas. The buildings and Lady Liberty still gave me that same distant stare, but I didn't care. I was home, almost. I'd written Addie, my sister, that I'd be comin' and hoped that she expected me. She met me at Union Depot, the train station in Chicago. We cried and hugged and laughed, and then suddenly she slapped me. She'd gotten the news of my death before my other letters arrived.

'Don't do that, don't ever do that again!' she scolded me through her tears.

'What?' I asked.

'Die,' she said. Then she kissed my cheek and said, 'Come on, Frank, dinner's waiting.' We went home to her place. She asked me what I was gonna do now and what a fool I was for playin' this game. I told her I'd change it all back. I'd say that we got switched somehow on the battlefield and, because of my injuries and state of mind during my hospital stay, I didn't know the difference. I'm sure it happens. I'd take care of it. Babies get switched all the time.

'But babies don't do it,' she said.

'Have you heard from Helen?' I asked, wantin' to change the subject and also because I really wanted to know. Helen still ate at my heart and soul.

'No, she's been avoiding me, too,' Addie said sadly. 'Mother says she heard Lloyd's around a lot. Your—her boy had been sick, too, apparently.'

'Then I must see her and my boy.'

'Wouldn't it be better to write first? It's been a long time and things aren't the same.'

'She'd just tear my letter up. No, I must go.'

'Do you still love her?'

'Yes. I always will.'

'Then go you must. Perhaps she still loves you.' I thought about seein' Helen after all that time. I thought about my buddies in France, too.

'Where's Oak Park?' I asked.

'A few miles west of here. Why?'

'Nothin'.' I touched my face. 'How do I look?'

She looked at me seriously and gently touched my scars. 'Older...tired...hurt...but wiser? Here, let's see what we can do for you.' Then she got some of her theatre makeup and dabbed some on my face. I could hardly feel her fingers as she worked. My face was numb.

'There; what do you think?' She brought me to the mirror. I stood and gazed at my reflection.

'I guess it's better.' In truth I hardly recognized myself, and that frightened me.

30

"I took the train up the lake and over to Waukesha the next mornin'. Helen was still at her parents' from what Addie heard. I was wearin' some decent civilian clothes now that fit me. I walked around town some. It was strange bein' back home; everythin' was so quiet, so ordinary. It was too quiet, too ordinary. But I'd get used to it, I told myself over and over, as 'normal' life gently scraped away at my soul just like war did. I'd be all right; I'd learn to survive. I'd learned how ta kill, now I could unlearn it. I knew I could. I had to.

"I was hopin' that I might bump into Helen in town somewhere. I didn't wanna make a scene at her parents'. I didn't see her in any of the shops, but the people looked at me as if they knew me even though I knew they didn't. They gave me that same distant stare I'd gotten before shippin' out to war, that knowin', judgin' kind a look that people get when they see somethin' they don't understand but try to pretend they do. I wished they'd all mind their own damn business. They didn't know anything.

"The park down by the Fox River was nearby, so I headed there. It was a favorite spot of Helen's that she'd told me about, told me about when she used to tell me things like that. I sat on a bench at the top of the hill and looked down at the valley and river. I had a good view, and it was a pleasant day with the autumn colors startin' ta show. Then I saw Helen. She was walkin' along the promenade as she pushed a baby buggy. My God, she was more beautiful than ever as she bent to smile and talk to her little passenger, our child. Then she continued on; her long, soft hair pulled up high like was the fashion caught the afternoon sunshine. She was radiant. I was glad that she looked so well and so happy. I got up from my bench and slowly walked down the hillside toward her. I wanted to run, but I had to look inconspicuous, ordinary, calm, like anyone else. I just wanted to watch her for a while. She hadn't seen me yet when the baby cried and she stopped. Pickin' him up, she pacified and cooed to him as she looked out over the river. I came closer to them now, and she saw me out of the corner of her eye. She turned when I stopped, and she looked at me like she was thinkin' of a dream that she could hardly remember.

'Hello, Helen,' I said.

She just stared at first.

'I thought...no...I heard...,' she began.

'I know. Just wounded. It was a mistake, a misunderstanding. I'm alive.'

'Oh, Frank, oh my God, Frank...' she started to cry, and the baby did, too.

'May I?' I gestured to the baby. I wanted to see and hold him. She looked at me. 'It's all right. I just want...I just want to a minute.' She slowly put the infant in my arms but kept one hand tightly on the blanket. Her other hand settled on my arm.

"He was everything I'd imagined. He was perfect. He'd stopped cryin' now, and I just stared at his little face. Even then I could see he had his mother's dark eyes; there was somethin' about his nose and face that looked like me, the me that used to be. I smiled at him and touched his soft blonde hair. My eyes filled with tears and I began to cry. He smiled and gurgled.

'I named him Henry,' Helen said. 'No one suspected.' Henry was my real middle name. She smiled and wiped a tear from my cheekbone with her gentle hand.

'I'm so sorry, Helen...'

'Don't be sorry. I'm sorry.'

'Is he...?' I needed to know for sure if he was mine.

'Yes, of course he is. I had to tell everyone he's Lloyd's. You have no idea how hard it's been.' She broke down again.

'I'd like to. I want to know. I love you, Helen.'

'God, Frank, please. Don't make this harder for me. I'm engaged. I thought you were killed!'

"Then we sat and she told me what'd happened over the last year. Lloyd made her life a livin' hell and refused to divorce her. He said she had to come back to him or he would destroy her career and take away her baby. He said he'd prove she was an unfit mother and make her pay for her infidelities. Only recently did she get the divorce after meetin' a new man that her father knew in town. He was a young lawyer named Bernard Jensen. Afterward, he'd proposed. She knew he truly loved her, and even though she wouldn't say that she truly loved him, she cared for him enough and knew she needed his support, especially for our child.

'Don't you love me anymore?' I asked her softly. She turned and looked away across the river. The white afternoon clouds cast a shadow across the glistenin' water that cut into the opposite bank and beyond.

'Yes, Frank. I always will. But I can't marry you.'

'Why?'

'It just wouldn't work. How could it?' She was becoming angry. 'My parents blame you, Frank, but everyone else blames me. I blame myself. You want me to turn my back on my family, too? I just want peace...just peace.' I hated to see her cry again.

"I walked with her a little further and asked if I could walk her home. She said no; even though her parents were out of town, it wouldn't be appropriate. Too many people might have seen us already, and when people see, people talk. We were alone when I tried to kiss her, but she pulled away.

'Then goodbye, Helen. I wish you well.'

'Goodbye, Frank. Please take care of yourself. Say hello to Addie?'

"I watched her walk up the street and turn the corner. Then she was gone. I stayed in town 'til it got dark and decided to take one last walk past her house. I wanted to see how she looked, happy, safe and content inside the brightly lit rooms. Lit houses always look good in the dark. I wanted to make sure they were well. I blamed myself for everything.

"In the dark a man walked up to the front door as I stood across the street by a tree. He let himself in. I thought it was her new fiancé, so I followed and quietly came up to the house so that I might see what he looked like. I could hear raised voices, even from the porch, and when I carefully looked in a window, I could see Helen's tearful and frightened face across the room, and then I recognized the back of the beast. It was Lloyd. I went insane with rage and strode to the door. It was still open so I entered to witness the drama that was takin' place. I froze.

"Lloyd was holdin' the child in one arm with a knife in the other hand. Helen was on her knees now, pleadin' with him to stop. He was stunned to see me and quickly drew the curtains closed.

'Well, if it isn't Soldier Boy come back from the dead,' he quietly said. Without a word I pulled out my Colt 45, the war pistol that was in my jacket, and calmly aimed it at him. I don't remember why I had it. Habit, maybe. Maybe I knew there might be trouble.

'What happened? The devil didn't want ya either?' He laughed a drunken laugh.

'No, Frank!' Helen screamed.

'Put that down or the baby gets his,' Lloyd spewed. I looked at Helen as she nodded with her eyes closed. Her tears hit the floor below her.

'He's not your baby, he's...' I began, tryin' to reason with him.

'Well, all the more reason then,' he hissed.

"I should have shut up, but it didn't matter now. 'Don't be stupid, Lloyd, you'll never get away with this,' I said, about to toss my gun.

'Stupid? Uh, uh. And you're not such a dumb kid, after all. Hand it over slow, right here, put it right here.' I carefully set the pistol down on the table next to 'im.

'Now, go in there,' he directed as he motioned us into the first floor bedroom. 'This is where you wanna be, anyway,' he taunted. After he shut and locked the door, I could hear him prop a chair under the knob on the outside. 'Don't move 'til I'm gone.' The baby was crying.

"I could hear Lloyd go out to the kitchen, and, as soon as he left the hall, I knocked the bedroom door in and ran to the back. He was still in the kitchen, fumblin' with the locked back door. Now everything happened so fast. He dropped the baby and started to point the gun at me, but I grabbed it and we struggled. The gun hit the floor and I went to grab it. Lloyd just stood there, lookin' in the other room with a weird smile on his face, a leerin' smile with bad teeth. Then a shot rang out, and Lloyd fell back and went down. Helen was standin' in the hallway with a small gun in her hand. It was her father's from the desk drawer. She'd shot him dead.

31

"Do you need a break?" Melanie asked Dan. He looked and sounded tired.

"Yeah...a bit...and the mosquitoes are out. Let's go inside." We put Dan on the sofa, and I got us all a glass of lemonade. I put a straw in his, and he sipped it with his eyes closed while he rested. Melanie quietly perused the house, looking at its contents like a museum director evaluating an exhibit. It was in a time warp, no doubt. The walls were all painted mint green, except for the bathroom which was pink to match the flamingo tiles. The old metal blinds were bent behind the heavily patterned curtains. On the kitchen wall hung a painting of an old bearded man praying before a loaf of bread and a Bible. A beanbag ashtray sat on the coffee table. An electric clock marked time inside a mallard duck as it flew on the wall out of a cattail patch. Everything needed a good dusting.

"I'll talk to Angie about getting some cleaners in," I told Melanie. Angie was my supervisor for Dan. Why didn't I do it sooner, I asked myself? When Dan was in the hospital would have been an excellent time.

"She's on top of my dresser. Next to the cufflinks," Dan mumbled. Angie's on top of the dresser? What?

"What did you say?" I asked, wondering if Dan really was hallucinating now.

"Helen's photo. Look in my jewelry box. Next to the cufflinks is my watch. Would you bring it, please?"

"Sure," I said as I went to the bedroom. Melanie was already there looking around. She joined me by the bureau. Above it hung an old print of the Little Mermaid statue in Denmark. I hadn't really noticed it before, but somehow it looked familiar. Then I remembered my dream that night with Melanie: woman, rock, water. Did this have something to do with it? I opened the small, plain wooden box and was surprised to see how much was in there. I never thought of Dan ever wearing anything flashy before, but I guess he did once. Among the cufflinks and tie clips were old coins, U.S. and French, some old wristwatches and rings, and, in a separate compartment, a pocket watch with a pendant of the Virgin Mary on top. With it were some military clasps and bronze stars and two silver stars.

"Good things come in small packages," Melanie said. "Take it out." I cupped it in my hands, almost afraid to open it. It was an exquisite gold pocket watch with the initials FHL, for Frank Henry

Loudon, engraved on the tarnished metal. It was smooth and cool and fit in the palm of my hand. I carried it back to the living room, and we sat next to Dan.

"It's beautiful," I said.

"Now, it's yours," he said. "Go ahead; open it." I looked at it clumsily. I'd never used a pocket watch before, but I found the catch. It popped open, revealing a watch face with Roman numerals and the brand name Elgin. The inside of the lid was shiny bronze.

"Open the plate," he said with his eyes still closed. At the top of the plate was a tiny hasp. My short-nailed finger couldn't pop it so Melanie offered her thumbnail and unsnapped it but let me do the rest. The plate folded down, and there she was. Helen looked out at me like she'd been waiting since 1917 to say *Why, hello. I was wondering when you'd get here.* Her long chestnut hair was done up on her head, her big brown eyes looked slightly to the side, and a coy smile flirted on her full but closed lips. She was as lovely as Dan said. The old photo wasn't really black and white but more a subtle mixing of browns and beiges. I'd only seen one picture of my great-gram Ellie. She'd been much older, but I could see the similarities now. And there were even traits that I could see in myself.

"She's beautiful, Dan," said Melanie. I nodded. Dan got up and sat on the couch now.

"Thank you. I don't know what else to say," I offered.

"My pleasure. 'Bout time you two met." After a moment Melanie put her hand on Dan's arm.

"But the baby," Melanie asked. "What happened when Lloyd dropped the baby?"

"The child…was all right. By some miracle—or maybe out of some goodness left in Lloyd's heart—he'd landed in the laundry basket by the door. It was full of clothes and broke his fall. Helen still stood in a daze in the hallway as I went to pick up the child. He was cryin,' of course, but other than that, he looked unharmed. I brought him to Helen and went to take the gun from her hand when she snapped, 'Don't touch it!'

'Helen, he's dead…'

'Get out, Frank. They'll blame you for all the trouble. Now get out!'

'Helen, I can't leave you here to take the blame…'

'It was self-defense; it was my father's gun and I had the right to use it. Now leave before somebody comes.' Already, someone was pounding at the front door. Helen pushed me to the kitchen door. 'Now

90

go,' she said. I took my pistol and went out the back. I paused to look into her dark, desperate eyes one last time and was gone. It was still dark so I cut through some backyards and made my way around the edges of town. I passed a pond and threw my gun in. I never wanted to see a gun again.

"I took the train back to Chicago. Walkin' to Addie's, I saw a recruitin' poster for the Marines. It was the same one I'd seen when I joined up. It was tattered now, and someone had drawn a mustache on the pretty woman in the picture. Same as before, '*Want to fight? Join the Marines*', it still said. But I didn't feel like fightin' anymore. I was sick of fightin'. In a month 'The War to End All Wars' would be over. Roughly nine million people died. Never again, people kept sayin'. Thank God, never again.

"A few months later I took a cab to Oak Park. I wanted to visit my ol' chum Ernie Hemingway who I'd met overseas. We'd written a few times and he told me he was gonna be back in town soon. When I got to his home, I met his sister Marcelline who told me that he was at the library.

'How is he?' I asked her.

She thought a moment.

'Quieter, but just as troublesome. His legs are doing better.'

He was standin' at the checkout desk, talkin' to a pretty librarian when I arrived. I could tell he was flirtin' with her as she gazed into his dark eyes, soakin' up every word like he was Zeus or somethin'.

'Hi, Ernie.'

'Frank! How are ya?' He gave me a huge handshake. He was different when he was sober, almost like he was tryin' too hard. We went back to his home and had some tea in the parlor. He introduced me to his family, and we talked about the war. We both compared scars and swapped lies. I told him about losin' Helen. He said he'd lost a love, too, some nurse he'd met while recuperatin' in Italy. I didn't tell him about me becomin' someone else.

'Don't let her get away with it,' he said.

'What do you mean?' I asked.

'Dumping you.'

'What do you expect me to do, sue? I *killed* enough people already.'

'Make her look bad in a story, get it out. Do you wonders.' Then he looked at me as his face lit up. "Better yet, kill her off! Thanks, pal! I owe you another one." Then, he let out a short, loud, demonic laugh and picked up a pocket notebook from the side table and made some notes while he grinned. I didn't see how that would help anything, but he seemed thrilled.

'It's odd, isn't it, bein' back home?' I asked.

'Yeah, too quiet, except when my sisters are around.'

'What should we do for our next adventure?'

'Why don't you come up to our place in Michigan with me, near Petoskey? I have to give a talk up there soon. We can hunt and fish. We'll have a helluva good time. Whaddaya say?' I'd heard of Petoskey before. I once read an article about the last, surviving flock of passenger pigeons killed there in 1878. It was a massive slaughter, apparently, that the residents were proud of. Fifty thousand pigeons killed each day for five months. It was quite efficient and necessary, they believed, as the people were tired of livin' in a town covered with bird shit. I told him about it, but he didn't seem to recall hearin' about it.

'The last one died four years ago at the Cincinnati Zoo,' I said. 'Her name was Martha. She was twenty-nine.'

'Shame,' he said, shakin' his head. 'The last of one.'

"But I didn't feel like huntin' or fishin', so I suggested we go to my uncle's farm near Kenosha. Besides, it was a lot closer. My aunt was the best cook in the world, and we could help on the farm durin' the day, and at night go into town and get drunk and dance at the big dance hall there. Kenosha women were the best dancers and the best lookin', I said. He agreed to the plan, so we hobbled off down the street to a tavern as we sang, 'Kenosha-ing we go, Kenosha-ing we go, high-ho the derry-o, Kenosha-ing we go...'

"The next year, he even stayed with me for a time while he worked in Chicago. I introduced him to a young friend of Addies's. They married and moved away. I never saw Ernie again."

32

Dan said that the Waukesha police decided that Helen had every right to shoot Lloyd. He'd been known to cause problems before, and this was the straw to break the camel's back, so to speak. The baby was fine, and Helen married the young attorney. He died a year later of influenza. She eventually moved to Rockford, Illinois, where she raised her child and continued teaching. She then became the first woman chairperson of the state's education department. She never remarried. She always told her son that his father was killed in the war. She said he was a hero. She knew this to be true.

Dan was never the same after the war and continued to use the identity that he'd borrowed so long ago on that battlefield in France. I think he did it more as a tribute to a fine young soldier, who otherwise would have been lost to obscurity, and as a chance for redemption with a new life. Either way, he never regretted it and said he was honored to "live my life out as best I could in someone else's shoes."

Dan kicked around the country for a few years, trying various jobs, as he said, "seein' the country that I'd fought and died for." He finally settled in Batavia, Illinois, a small river town west of Chicago, so he could still see Addie but find some peace. That's where he got his job working at the park, his park, my park, the park with the monument to all those dead guys, the one with the green statue on it and all those green names surrounded by fragile red poppies. The $10,000 death benefit from the government for Frank Loudon went to Helen. He made sure of that. That way he could feel that he'd supported his son, even though Helen never asked for it.

I finally told my parents about Dan and his tale. My dad didn't act too surprised and said he vaguely remembered something like it that his own dad had told him, though never knew that "Old Dan the Walkin, Man," was his grandfather. Gee, I was glad that families could communicate so well. When I asked Dan why he hadn't told me or my dad sooner, he said that he didn't know at first, either. He only found out one day when I was a little kid, maybe three or four, and my grampa Hank took me to the park. Grampa and I had sat on a bench, and he'd told me things about my family, things that I didn't understand at the time. Dan had been working nearby and overheard what my grampa was telling me. He'd asked him a few friendly questions and, bingo, he knew who was sitting in front of him but never admitted so. It was just sheer, freakish, insane luck that he was now living just a few homes away from his boy and his boy and *his* boy. What could Dan do? You can't just walk up to strangers and say, 'Hi, I'm your old man that died in WWI.' So he tried the best he could to be near us, to care for us, to be a part of our family. No wonder I saw him everywhere. And though I didn't know it at the time, I think I needed to be near him, too.

33

Dan died a few months later just after his one hundred-and-eleventh birthday, making him the oldest living resident in Illinois. He died on Armistice Day, what we now call Veterans' Day. The Armistice for WWI was signed at 11 o'clock on the eleventh day of the eleventh month of 1918. Dan had now reached his 111th year on Earth. Later, I thought about how strange it all was. Was this all in the plans, or did Dan will himself to do it? It didn't matter; he'd made it. Now he had peace.

I'd arranged to have him honored in the city's parade, and there was to be a reception afterward with local dignitaries and a fine lunch and maybe even some old music from the different war eras. He'd looked forward to it for weeks. After I let myself in, I found Dan lying in his bed. He'd died in his sleep. In his hand were two letters. One was one he'd written recently, thanking me for all the help I'd given him, saying he was proud of me and loved me. The other was the last letter he'd received from Helen, the first one she'd sent him in over sixty years. She'd sent it to him thirty years ago, just a month before she died.

It read: *Dear Frank: Thank you for giving me the freedom to do as I wished all those years ago. I know I treated you badly, and the only regret that I have now is that our son didn't get to know you as the fine man that I knew you to be. I died the same day that you "died," Frank, and I was never the same. I don't think you would have loved me the same after that, even if you thought you could. Please forgive me for all the trouble I've caused you. And please know that, even though we've been apart, I have never let one day go by when I haven't thought of you, and loved you. Yours always, Helen.*

I was able to get Dan buried with full military honors. Later I wrote him a letter that I left in his coffin, just like he'd left one in that bird house for his sick friend Charles, all those years ago in France. I felt bad that I'd never told him I loved him, in person, but I knew he knew.

A commemorative plaque was placed at the veterans' home for all his years of faithful volunteering, and a bronze plate, this one shiny and new, was affixed to the WWI monument at the park. It read: *Frank Henry Loudon, aka Dan Marshall, Last Known Veteran of World War One, is honored here this day for his many years of dedicated service to his country, to his community, and to this park and this monument which he so carefully tended for over eighty years.*

I had Dan buried in Rockford, Illinois, right next to Helen and my grampa Hank. It was a scenic place, looking over the Rock River. As we left him there, I took one last glance at the engraved verse on the back of his headstone. I wondered if anyone but Melanie and I would even know what it meant. It read:

Good Morning Mr. Zip-Zip-Zip, with your haircut just as short as mine.

Good Morning Mr. Zip-Zip-Zip, you're surely looking fine—

On the drive home I asked Melanie when she was going to give me that test, the one for *The Old Man and the Sea* that she said I'd have to take before she decided to marry me.

"Oh, Tom," she said with a kiss. "Didn't you know? You passed it with flying colors." We married that spring; Melanie wore a red poppy in her hair. Dan would have been proud.

I gave Melanie one last surprise wedding gift as we made our way out of town in a limo taking us to our favorite state park lodge for a quiet honeymoon. The gift was actually something Dan had mentioned to me months earlier; I'd forgotten about it and I'd found in his closet after he'd passed. It was already wrapped in brown paper as a wedding gift for us. I guess he was just sure it was going to happen. I knew Melanie'd like it so I saved it special for now.

"Here," I said, "Something for us from Dan." She was genuinely surprised. I'd kept it hidden.

"What is it?"

"I'm not sure, exactly. Some old manuscript, I think, that a friend gave him a long time ago." Her mouth began to open. "Nothing ever came of it, apparently."

"D-Did this friend's name happen to be *Ernie*?" She said this very slowly, quietly.

"Yeah, why?" Her eyes started to glaze as she unwrapped the parcel.

"Oh-my-God...Tommy!"

95

Epilogue

Most people get to know their family all their lives. Some never know who their family is. I was lucky to find part of mine, if only for a short while. I catch myself spending more time at the park lately, and Melanie and I volunteer at the vets' home once a week. It's a nice stroll. I think of Dan often in so many ways as I walk around my little town. I try to see things the way he did. And even though I know him to be my great-grandfather by another name, he'll always be "Old Dan the Walkin' Man" to me. I'd known him all my life. He was everywhere. He was the Last of One.

About the Author

Stephan Solberg has lived in the Chicago area all his life and comes from a family of teachers: his father was a history teacher, his wife is an English teacher, their daughter Sara is an art teacher, and their son Daniel is a college vocal coach. Besides being a writer, Steve has been an artist, a realtor, a landscape designer, and a park service worker. He sings a mean Frank Sinatra and can sometimes be seen twirling his wife on the dance floor to a country rhythm. He is currently working on a short story collection as well as a novel set in the Indiana Dunes. This is his first novel.